Band Geeked Out

For my family,
who have always been there to help me figure it out.

Band Geeked Out

josie bloss

Woodbury, Minnesota

First Edition
First Printing, 2009

Book design by Steffani Sawyer
Cover design by Lisa Novak
Cover image © 2009 Tony Anderson/Iconica/Getty Images

Flux, an imprint of Llewellyn Publications

Library of Congress Cataloging-in-Publication Data

Bloss, Josie, 1981–
  Band geeked out / Josie Bloss.—1st ed.
      p. cm.
  Sequel to: Band geek love.
  Summary: As her senior year of high school nears the end, marching band member Ellie finds herself doubting her plans for the future when she meets a fascinating and sophisticated girl while taking a tour of a college out of state.
  ISBN 978-0-7387-1469-1
  [1. Identity—Fiction. 2. College choice—Fiction. 3. Interpersonal relations—Fiction. 4. Marching bands—Fiction. 5. Bands (Music)—Fiction. 6. High schools—Fiction. 7. Schools—Fiction.] I. Title.
  PZ7.B6238Bap 2009
  [Fic]—dc22
                                                          2008048703

Flux
Llewellyn Publications
A Division of Llewellyn Worldwide, Ltd.
2143 Wooddale Drive, Dept. 978-0-7387-1469-1
Woodbury, MN 55125-2989, U.S.A.
www.fluxnow.com

Printed in the United States of America

Acknowledgments

My never-ending gratitude goes out to the following: Kate Schafer Testerman, my fantastically supportive agent; Andrew Karre, Brian Farrey, and everyone at Flux for expertly holding my hand through this second-book adventure; Adam Schweigert, who knew how to make the story interesting; everyone at the Bloomington Playwrights Project, for giving me a fabulous creative outlet; Dad and Sue, for all their amazing support; and Mom and Mark, for helping me wrestle this book into submission on that long car ride up to the Keweenaw.

Thank you all … you're the best!

Also by Josie Bloss

Band Geek Love

One

My mom left the thick envelope on the corner of the library table in the entryway, where she knew I would see it the moment I came home from jazz band practice.

"Ellie, something came for you today from Covington," she called from the kitchen, before I even had a chance to say hello. "Let me know what it says, okay?"

Heart pounding like the biggest bass drum, I gingerly picked up the envelope by the corner and escaped up to my room. I sat at my desk and stared at it.

The envelope appeared benign enough ... just an ordinary off-white envelope, a little thick around the middle like it might hold several pieces of paper.

Maybe even a whole *packet*.

A packet of paper meant a big problem and was also why I stared at it for twenty minutes without touching it, like I was afraid the envelope contained anthrax or something. Because if the envelope held more than one piece of paper, that meant it was probably an acceptance packet. And an acceptance packet meant that I had somehow gotten into my mom's alma mater, Covington College, an elite women's liberal arts school in rural New York.

Very, *very* far away from my home in the middle of Michigan.

Which meant I would have to actually choose.

My mom called up the stairs, "Did you open it yet? What did it say?"

"I'm busy, *Mom!*" I yelled back.

"Well … let me know when you open it!" I could tell she was frustrated. She'd been waiting for this envelope probably even more than I had.

I decided to go into momentary denial, and got up and started pacing around the room, pausing to pick things up and put them down again at random. I did a few yoga stretches. I took my trumpet out of its case and doodled a few phrases from the music we'd played at jazz band practice. I stood at my dresser mirror and picked at a spot on my chin until it was an attractive shade of angry pink.

Stuck on my dresser mirror was a sappy picture of my boyfriend Connor and me, taken on Valentine's Day. More than a month ago. I had wrangled myself into a dark brown dress and Connor was dapper in a black suit, his arm around my shoulder, his face half in my hair and both of our faces beaming and shiny.

That had been the first night he'd said "I love you" out loud.

Above the picture was a bumper sticker from the state university here in Michigan where I was already accepted for this fall and where, up until I received this suspiciously thick envelope from Covington, I was almost certain I would be going after graduation. I had even already sent in the $250 enrollment deposit.

These two things—my beloved boyfriend and State— were pretty much synonymous in my mind. Like peanut butter and jelly. Melodies and harmonies.

Just two nights ago, Connor and I had discussed that fact as we sat alternately talking and making out in my car. We were parked in front of where Connor lives (with his uncle, who also just happens to be our band director, Mr. Barr), delaying the inevitable moment when he would have to go in.

"It won't be *so* bad when you're at State," Connor had said from someplace near my right ear, his hand creeping like a warm spider over my stomach. "It's only a twenty minute drive. We'll probably see each other all the time."

I had sighed, and leaned closer so that his face and mouth were pressed against my neck. "Yeah, I know, but it won't be the same. I won't be with you everyday. I won't sit next to you in symphonic band, or see you in the halls, or have lunch with you, or—"

Connor cut me off, pulling my face around toward his for one of his long, heart-pounding kisses that never failed to leave me breathless. We had been dating for seven months, which sometimes felt like approximately forever in high school time, but I could still live and die and be born again in those kisses of his. I couldn't imagine a time when I *wouldn't*.

I mean, look at all he'd done for me: Pulled me out of my shell when no other guy would come near me, gave me my first shivery kiss in the movie theater during *The Wizard of Oz*, forgiven me when I went on to accidentally kiss someone else, and probably (though I hadn't pinned him down on it) threw his symphonic band audition back in November to make sure I got first chair.

Like any good boyfriend would do.

It didn't even bother me anymore that he was almost definitely better than me at trumpet, nor that he was almost definitely cuter than me on the objective scale of high school hotness (just ask all the popular, pretty girls at Winslow High who still can't believe a band geek like me grabbed him).

All that mattered was that he loved me, and I loved him, and that somehow we worked together.

"Maybe that will make the chances we do have to see each other even better," Connor suggested, pulling back after a delicious moment. "You know, like delayed gratification or something."

I shrugged and leaned in for more of the warm-mouthed kissing, trying to forget that I'd be going away to college in a mere five months, while he would still be here in Winslow.

In high school. Without me. For two more years.

And *that* sort of angst had occurred when I still thought there wasn't any chance that I'd get into long-shot Covington, which was approximately ten and a half hours away by car (I Google-mapped it—several times—hoping the estimate would magically change).

I had really applied to Covington just in order to humor my mom, who somehow thought that in this time of ultra-competitive applications, where high school seniors have to be student council president, valedictorian, head of the yearbook, and save endangered sea turtles over every spring break since fifth grade in order to be accepted anywhere selective, that *I* would have any chance of getting into a place like Covington.

I mean, I'm pretty smart and have a good GPA and all, but I'm not what you would call extracurricularly exceptional. Band was basically my only hobby, and I couldn't imagine schools like Covington—where they obviously didn't even have a football team, let alone a *marching band*—would be all that impressed with that sort of pastime.

Which is why State made so much sense. I could go there and fit right into a fantastic college band like a bright white dress glove.

And, perhaps coolest of all, both of my best friends had already been accepted at State also. Against all odds, Kristen had gotten her grades up enough during fall semester to meet the GPA requirement. And Jake, who had been drum major at Winslow, was practically *predestined* to become the drum major for a giant university marching band. That wouldn't be for a few years yet, but the boy had the talent and we all knew it was going to happen.

The three of us had been planning on going to college together since we'd received our acceptance letters a month ago. We'd have each other to lean on once we got there and it wasn't so scary, then, thinking about leaving home.

It had all seemed so easy and obvious until...

I glanced over at my desk, irrationally hoping that maybe the envelope would have vanished or become spontaneously rejection-letter skinny. But there it was. Looking full and thick and just ever so slightly bent, as if someone had tried to read through the envelope.

My mom, no doubt. I wouldn't be surprised if she'd steamed the envelope open just to find out as soon as possible. In the past few months, it had become her absolute fondest dream that I go to elite Covington.

"Just think, Ellie," she'd said at least four or thirty-five times in the past week alone. "*Covington*. Did you know that two Pulitzer prize-winning journalists and four state supreme court judges have graduated from there? That almost all of their programs are top ranked? And that the campus is recognized as one of the most beautiful in the country?"

And I'd sighed and rolled my eyes, all four or thirty-five times.

"Yeah, *Mom*, you've mentioned that."

She didn't acknowledge the sarcasm.

"Really, it doesn't even compare to State, don't you think? That it's in an entirely different league, I mean?"

My mom loves to phrase her opinions as questions. I'm pretty sure she thinks it makes them less offensive to whomever she's talking to.

I had merely shaken my head. It wasn't just that my parents were snobs about where I received my higher education (they *totally* were), but they also knew what me going to State meant.

Because the program to which I had applied, auditioned for, and been accepted to was music education. My current life plan was to go to State, be in the 300-person marching band, and eventually become a high school band director.

It just made sense to me, in the same way it makes sense that the sky is blue and chocolate is delicious. I loved everything about band ... why *shouldn't* I pursue it as a career?

Though my parents had semi-graciously tolerated my high school involvement in band, it wasn't surprising that me being just-a-band-director was not what they had envisioned for my forever-future.

"Why would you want to commit to that path when you're so young?" Mom kept asking, throwing her hands up. "There's plenty of time for you to go get a Master's degree in music education later on, after you experience *other* things, if that's what you really want. I think you should focus on being in school, and learning a wide variety of subjects. You're just so good at English … and science. And aren't you ready to try a new sort of extracurricular activity? Something *besides* band? Don't you think there are better ways to spend your time now that you're almost an adult?"

There was that opinion-as-question thing again.

"Mom, I *love* band," I'd said. "We've been over this a million times. Besides, what about the scholarship? I have a good shot at getting a full ride at State and you know it. Wouldn't that make things so much easier?"

Every year, a private alumni fund associated with State offered one full-ride scholarship to an incoming freshman who was committed to pursuing music education. It was based on an additional audition—my spring solo recital, over a month from now—but I was confident I was a strong candidate.

Trumpet playing was my *thing*, after all.

No matter how much my parents wanted to deny it.

"I just don't want you to get caught in a rut, and have college be just like high school," Mom said with a sigh. "Dad and I have put away money for your education and you're *lucky* that you don't have to worry about student loans or working your way through school like we did. And if you go to State and just do basically the same thing as in high school, how will you really grow and expand? How will you know that's really what you want to do if you don't experience lots of different things?"

I didn't reply to that, as it was slightly too similar to my own quiet, unvoiced concerns about going to State. Concerns I'd barely allowed to be spoken within the confines of my own head. That maybe I was just being a coward by going to a university nearby—where it would sort of be like high school again, only bigger.

Because hadn't I *hated* high school? Hadn't I been looking forward to graduating since the first day of freshman year? Shouldn't I *want* to go far away?

Instead of thinking too hard, though, I latched on to another one of my default retorts. "Maybe I *want* to help pay for my own college, maybe that's *important* to me. Didn't you guys always teach me that I should be responsible for myself?"

Before she could reply, I continued. "And why do you want me to go so far away from Winslow, anyhow? Covington is a whole day's drive from here. If I went to State, you'd probably see me every week. I'd be able to come back here to do my laundry. Are you sick of me or something? Do you *want* me to be on the other side of the country? Are you *trying* to get rid of me?"

Mom looked at me with big, moist eyes.

"Of course not. I'd love to have you nearby. But I just want … the best for you. That's all Dad and I both want, Ellie. And we're just not convinced that becoming a band director is the right path...we think you're meant for more."

Which was the core problem here, without a doubt. I was supposed to make them proud by going off to become a doctor or a United Nations official or a lawyer for Legal Aid like my dad or something.

My parents couldn't deal with the fact that their precious only child just wanted to be a band geek for the rest of her life.

I stood up. "Well, how about what makes *me* happy? Did you ever think of that?"

I used that as my dramatic exit line to escape the kitchen and the endless ripples of tension and anxiety between my mom and me.

Because, in general, things with my parents had been all right for the past few months...better than they'd been for most of high school, anyway. They had calmly accepted my relationship with Connor and hadn't been harassing me about who I was hanging out with or how I was spending my time.

Unless we were talking about college (more specifically, Covington), we got along fine. You wouldn't even realize there was a giant navy-blue-and-white (Covington's colors) elephant trampling around the house, knocking over vases.

I continued circling the envelope in my room like a very nervous, toothy shark. Mom was still in the kitchen, loudly rattling things around, and I knew she was impatient. Dad would be home soon, too, and then it would be all over.

"Just open it, silly girl," I snapped at myself. "You need to know one way or the other. You need to deal with it."

So finally, with shaking hands, I picked up the envelope and tore along the top with my finger. The edge caught the soft skin of the inside of my index finger and gave me a sharp paper cut. A spot of bright red blood was left on the creamy paper inside.

"Oh, that's just *great*," I muttered, putting the wound to my mouth and sucking on it.

With my other hand, I took out the contents of the envelope, which was definitely a packet of papers. Not *one* piece of paper that regretfully informed me of anything. I took my finger out of my mouth and unfolded the sheets slowly, putting aside the postage-paid envelope that was included. I took a deep breath and read the first words:

We are delighted to inform you that Covington wishes to extend an offer of admission!

I didn't read any more. I set the papers back down on my desk and crept into my bed, still fully clothed, and pulled the comforter over my head.

Two

C-NOTE: HEY CUTIE... HOW'S IT GOING?

TRUMPETGRRL: ...

C-NOTE: ????

C-NOTE: IS EVERYTHING OKAY?

TRUMPETGRRL: WELL, DEPENDS ON HOW YOU
LOOK AT IT. I GOT A LETTER TODAY...

TRUMPETGRRL: FROM A CERTAIN SCHOOL...

C-NOTE: COVINGTON??

TRUMPETGRRL: YEP.

C-NOTE: AND?

TRUMPETGRRL: SEEMS TO BE THAT I GOT IN.

Connor didn't reply immediately, and I stared anxiously at the computer screen. I really should have just sacked up and told him in person, I decided. This not being able to see his face stuff was giving me ulcers.

The seconds dragged on torturously... I gnawed at my thumbnail.

What was Connor doing? *Crying* or something? I mean, he *was* a particularly sensitive guy but I really didn't want to be responsible for that and—

C-Note: Sorry, my cousin was asking me
   something.
C-Note: Els, that's great you got in! I'm so
   proud of you!

Um, what?

He was *proud* of me? No immediate deep, devastating depression over the fact I might not be around next year? No instant admonishments that I could never ever leave him not ever or he might wither away and *die?* He thought it was GREAT that I got in a college three states away?

What the hell!?

TrumpetGrrl: Um ... thanks.
C-Note: I bet your parents are happy about
   it.
TrumpetGrrl: Yeah, they're pretty excited.
   But, you know ...

TrumpetGrrl: Just because I got in doesn't
mean I HAVE to go or anything.

I was quite frankly quite amazed that I had to *remind* him
of this fact. Did he *want* me to go far away? Did everyone
just want me gone out of their lives? Was I really such a
terrible trial of a person?

C-Note: Well, sure, but it's still cool that
you got in. It's a great school.
TrumpetGrrl: YEAH I KNOW THAT
THANKS.

There was a pause, and I could perfectly envision him sitting at his computer with his forehead wrinkled in confusion. With the same bewildered expression he always had
when he couldn't figure me out.

Which wasn't as often as it used to be anymore, but
still happened on occasion.

Seriously, though. Was the boy *completely* clueless?

C-Note: Okay, what's wrong?
TrumpetGrrl: Forget it. Nothing.
C-Note: Don't do that. What is it? Tell me.

I sighed loudly, like he could hear me through the computer.

TrumpetGrrl: Well, for ONE, they want to take me on a trip there.

C-Note: Your parents? To Covington? What's wrong with that?

TrumpetGrrl: What's WRONG is that I DON'T WANT TO GO THERE.

C-Note: Then what does it hurt going to take a look?

See, this is why Connor and I make such a good couple. I freak out, and he says something simple and obvious and completely defuses the situation. Even in the midst of my intense annoyance at him and at my parents and at pretty much the entire world, I could appreciate that.

But still, couldn't he see that nothing good would come out of me going to visit? I was *supposed* to go to State. I was *supposed* to go stick with the plan.

C-Note: What's your big problem with just making them happy with this one sorta small thing?

I rubbed my temples with my palms.

My parents had been beyond excited, of course, when I'd showed them the Covington acceptance letter. I'd waited until Dad came home from work and then sidled into the kitchen, casual-like, as if nothing of note had happened that day.

My mom immediately wheeled around from where she was pouring wine and searched my face. "So?"

I shrugged. "I got accepted at Covington."

Dad gave a big whoop and hugged me tight, and my mom kissed my forehead and told me how *wonderful* it was and how *proud* they were of me... how *impressed* they were that I got in.

You would have thought that I'd never done a decent thing in my entire life before the moment I got that letter.

"We'll go visit," Dad had said eagerly, grabbing his ever-present day planner from his briefcase. "So you can see the campus!"

"Great idea!" Mom said. "I'll get some time off and we'll go for a long weekend. You'll love it there, Ellie. Once you see it, you'll know. You just have to give it a chance."

"But..." I started. And then I looked at their happy, excited faces. They hadn't looked anything like that when I told them I got into State.

Which had been more of a casual "Oh, that's nice," kind of reaction.

> TRUMPETGRRL: I DUNNO. I JUST DON'T WANT
>   TO GO VISIT. IT'S STUPID AND POINTLESS AND
>   A WASTE OF TIME.
> C-NOTE: BUT IT'D MAKE YOUR PARENTS HAPPY,
>   RIGHT? WHY NOT? AND A FREE TRIP?

I rolled my eyes. It's not like it was a vacation in Cancún or anything.

TRUMPETGRRL: I GUESS. WHATEVER. WHO CARES.

C-NOTE: WELL, I'D GO IF I WERE YOU. JUST
HUMOR THEM. WHAT DOES IT MATTER IF YOU
DON'T ACTUALLY WANT TO GO THERE?

I pursed my lips and minimized the chat window to go check my email and refresh Facebook and, basically, do anything but think about the fact that my boyfriend was supporting my parents in wanting me to look at a school that was hundreds of miles away. Instead of only fifteen miles away. Like we had *discussed*.

After a few minutes, the chat window started blinking at the bottom of my screen.

C-NOTE: STILL THERE? YOU'RE NOT MAD, ARE
YOU?

I let him stew for another minute, and then replied.

TRUMPETGRRL: I DON'T KNOW.

C-NOTE: DON'T BE MAD. PLEASE...

C-NOTE: IT JUST DOESN'T SEEM RIGHT FOR YOU
TO NOT EVEN GIVE COVINGTON A CHANCE.

C-NOTE: I MEAN, I FEEL LIKE YOU'RE NOT EVEN
CONSIDERING IT BECAUSE OF ME...

C-NOTE: AND I DON'T WANT TO HOLD YOU
BACK.

And suddenly, I was crying. Seriously, one second I was fine and the next second, fat tears were dripping down my face as if a frozen pipe had burst in each of my eyeballs.

And the worst part was, I didn't even know *why* I was crying. Because I somehow got accepted by an ultra-competitive school? Because I had a sweet boyfriend who just wanted the best for me? Because my parents were supportive and wanted me to go to a good college? Because I had a tendency to be a selfish bitch to the people who loved me?

> TRUMPETGRRL: I KNOW THAT YOU DON'T WANT TO HOLD ME BACK. YOU'RE NOT.
> TRUMPETGRRL: AND I'M SORRY.
> C-NOTE: IT'S OKAY.

Connor is nothing if not forgiving. He sort of had to be, with me around.

I wiped the tears away with the heel of my palm and took a deep breath.

> TRUMPETGRRL: SO YOU REALLY THINK I SHOULD GO VISIT?
> C-NOTE: YES.
> TRUMPETGRRL: BUT WHAT IF I LIKE IT THERE?
> C-NOTE: THEN IT WILL HELP YOU MAKE A MORE INFORMED DECISION.
> TRUMPETGRRL: BUT I ALREADY MADE MY DECISION. I'M GOING TO STATE.

C-Note: Like I said, if you're so certain, then taking a look at Covington won't hurt anything. Give it a chance, Ellie.

"*Ugh*," I burst out to the screen. There just wasn't a point in arguing with these people anymore. They were all like a bunch of broken records, skipping perpetually on *Give it a chance! It won't hurt! Give it a chance! It won't hurt!*

The thing was, some part of me was insisting that visiting Covington *would* end up hurting.

Three

Well, I could count on at least one person reacting appropriately to the Covington news.

"Ellie, *no!*" said my best friend Kristen, like she was talking to a dog who had tracked mud across a white carpet. It was the next day, after symphonic band rehearsal, and I'd found her in the instrument storage room and given her the news. "You are *totally* not allowed to go to Covington. We all agreed we're going to State and we're going to be in marching band and you're going to be my roommate and it's going to be perfect, and therefore you're not allowed to go to Covington. We...we won't *let* you."

The "we" she was referring to was herself and her boyfriend, Jake, who was my other best friend. Kristen and Jake had started going out in the fall, right around the same time Connor and I had gotten together. Jake, Kristen, and I had been close since ninth grade, so I sort of understood what she was feeling.

Now she crossed her arms and looked at me with raised eyebrows, as if double-dog daring me to disagree with her.

"Dude, I *know*," I said. "I sure as hell don't want to go to Covington. But everyone seems to think that now I've gotten in I should at least visit—"

"Why?" Kristen burst in. "It's a stupid pointless waste of time!"

"That's what *I* said!" I told her. "They don't care."

"Ellie, you *have* to go to State." Her voice was getting shrill. "I'll *die* if you don't go there with me. And ... and so will Jake! He'll never forgive you."

"Won't forgive her for what?" asked Jake, coming into the storage room, probably to see why we hadn't come out yet.

"*She* is abandoning us!" Kristen said dramatically, pointing at me. "Tell Jake how you're ruining *everything*, Ellie."

I sighed loudly. "I'm not abandoning you!" I looked at Jake. "I got into Covington and now my parents want to go visit but—" I glared at Kristen, "that *doesn't* mean I'm actually going there next year. I'm just checking it out to make my parents happy."

And also, apparently, to make my stupid boyfriend happy, as screwed up and wrong as that was.

"You got into Covington?" Jake looked impressed. "Wow, that's awesome. Congratulations!"

With a frustrated grunt, Kristen hauled off and socked him in the arm.

"Ow! What the hell?"

"Jake, I can't believe you're supporting this," Kristen snapped.

"I'm not!" he said, rubbing his arm. "It's just really cool that she got in there, that's all. It's a really selective school, you know."

"Don't you dare encourage her!"

"I'm not, I'm just saying it's cool! Calm down!"

I felt like they were pseudo-parents arguing over my head.

"Kristen, seriously, I don't want to go there," I said, raising my hands between them so they'd shut up. "Don't worry. I'll just go on this trip and take a look and say it's not for me. All right? I'm going to State, just like we planned."

Her lower lip was pouted out. "You *promise?*"

"Pinky swear," I said, holding out my little finger. She linked her pinky finger with mine and we shook our hands up and down.

"Okay, just remember this," she said, holding on and bending my finger back just far enough so that it started to hurt. "Just remember this when you visit and meet a bunch of smart girls who tell you that you belong at some snobby East Coast school. Remember that you pinkysweared with me, Ellie! I promise I will hunt you down and kick your ass if you forget!"

"I will, I will," I said, ripping my finger away from her grip. "Jeez. You're so violent today, Kris."

"Well, apparently, everyone around here needs some sense smacked into them," she replied loftily. "That's all."

And with one last glare, she left the room.

Jake was looking at me with amusement.

"What's so damn funny?" I snapped.

"Oh, nothing," he said. "Just..."

"What? Out with it!"

"Just that I can't believe you're actually going to visit," he said, shaking his head. "You know what's going to happen, right?"

"No," I said, petulantly.

"You're probably going to love it," he said. "It'll be cool and new and interesting and not in Michigan and it's going to screw with your head."

"Who died and made you my personal psychic-friend network?" I snapped.

Jake shook his head, still with that irritatingly superior smile on his face. "Watch, you'll see, Ellie."

I frowned and felt worry wash over me. What if he was right?

"So, do you think I shouldn't go, then? I mean, should I not even look?"

Jake considered. "Yeah, I think you should at least look. Because you'll probably regret it if you don't. You'll always wonder if it would have been better. If that's the place you were supposed to go."

"But what if you're right? What if I like it so much that I don't want to go to State anymore?" All the insecurities I had about people apparently being *oh just fine* with me going far away came flooding back and I started to feel panicky. "Don't *you* want to go to college with me, Jake?" I asked, in small voice.

He rolled his eyes. "Of course I do, Els. I know it'd be a blast for the three of us to hang out together for another four years. But then again, we're only eighteen, right? And you're so freakin' smart...you might belong at a place like Covington, you know? With all the other freakin' smart girls?"

I looked down and blushed. Compliments from everything-is-a-joke Jake were few and far between, which made them that much more unexpected and sort of...precious.

"I suppose," I said, after a moment. "I mean, I don't suppose I'm that smart, but that I should at least go and look. You're right."

He gave me a friendly half-hug and walked toward the door. "Give it a chance, dude."

"That's what they all say," I muttered.

I dawdled as much as I could while putting away my trumpet, but Connor was still waiting for me in the band room when I came out. I'd managed to avoid talking to him for most of the day, still annoyed at how he'd acted online the night before.

All through symphonic band rehearsal he'd been try-ing to catch my eye, which had been really hard to ignore considering we sat right next to each other. I was first chair trumpet and he was second chair and our plas-tic seats were, literally, about six inches away from each other (depending on how zealous the night custodian had been with the mopping). But I had stared at my music and watched Mr. Barr intently and nudged Connor away when he tried to whisper in my ear.

Connor didn't wait for me to say anything when I appeared out of the locker room, but just put his long arms around me and pulled me close. Despite my annoy-ance, I couldn't help automatically inhaling the warm, familiar smell of his clothes and his skin ... this nice boy who for some reason put up with me and my craziness.

I began to feel teary again. How could I possibly con-sider leaving him behind?

"So, how are you?" he asked, pulling back and looking at my face.

I shrugged.

"I know you're pissed," he said. "Can we talk about it?"

I shrugged again and crossed my arms, putting space between us. Unlike most high school guys, Connor was a big fan of talking things out. Even if *I* didn't particularly feel like it.

"Okay, fine," he said. "I'll just ask you stuff and you reply with shrugs or nods, all right?"

Shrug.

"Is everything okay *other* than this college stuff?"

I considered, and then slowly nodded.

"So, are you going to visit Covington?"

I shrugged, and then nodded.

"Cool," he said. "I'm glad. I really think you're doing the right thing."

I sighed and leaned forward so my head was lying on his chest. He reached around to rub my back, strong fingers kneading at the knots under my shoulder blades.

"Don't worry so much, Els, or you'll drive yourself crazy," he said, and kissed the top of my head. "It's totally not as bad as you think."

Four

So is everyone all plugged in?" Dad asked, far too cheerfully considering it was five o'clock in the morning on a Friday. Which made it a full hour and forty-five minutes before when I usually got up for school. This was totally not the way I had envisioned spending the end of my Spring Break.

Kristen and Jake had gone on a road trip to Florida with some other band seniors, Connor had gone back to his hometown to hang out with his old friends and I was ... in the car with my parents to go spend time thinking about *school*.

"I'm set to go!" Mom chirped. "Ellie?"

I just moaned from the back seat, still not able to completely open my eyes. "Too. Early. Crazies."

"What are you talking about? This is the best part of the day," Dad said, deftly backing out of the driveway and simultaneously taking a large chug of coffee. He regularly got up at this time to go to his job at Legal Aid. I personally viewed it as a sickness. "Early bird gets the worm, my dear. That's something you'll have to learn ... well, probably not in college, but definitely in the working world."

In response, I yanked my iPod out of my backpack, inserted the earbuds, and burrowed my face into my pillow. I often thought the thing I was most looking forward to in college was not having any obligations before 10:00 AM. That was how life was *supposed* to be.

I woke in Ohio, and watched the passing scenery. Each mile marker reminded me I was getting further away from home, from Connor, from the plans I'd already made and had thought were set in stone.

The landscape became increasingly more lovely as we passed through Pennsylvania and got closer to the small New York town of Covington. There were rolling hills, and brief views of shimmering lakes, and budding trees just sending out their first fragile green leaves.

I found myself half in love with the land, with how different it was then flat, cornfield-covered central Michigan.

Not that Michigan isn't pretty but, you know, sometimes different is good.

We stopped at a gas station on the outside of town and I got out. I took a deep breath of the cool, fresh air and thought, stupidly, *This is the air that I could be breathing everyday.*

Yeah, I know. It was kind of melodramatic even for me.

Mom directed Dad through the center of the town, pointing out where her favorite places were.

"And that restaurant had the best coffee, and I used to study in the town library over there and ... oh, and that store is where you'll buy a lot of your books, Ellie." She glanced at me in the rearview mirror. "I mean, if you end up coming here."

I nodded, trying to look casually disinterested. "It's very ... small," I observed.

Covington was a cute little village, with brightly colored storefronts and flowering trees and a square in the middle with bike paths and a bubbling fountain.

Mom turned around in her seat. "See, Ellie, you could ride your bike here ... it's a very bike-friendly town! I rode my bike everywhere. Isn't that nice?"

"They have bike paths at State, too," I muttered half-heartedly.

But the truth was, Covington was nothing like State, which had attached itself like a giant barnacle to a sprawling suburban Michigan neighborhood of strip malls and traffic and parking lots. I mean, State and the town in which it was located weren't hideous or anything ... it had pretty trees and open spaces and cool old buildings, but it was still just regular, ordinary, humongous State.

While Covington looked self-contained, and sweet, and almost suspiciously like a movie set.

Band, I reminded myself firmly. As in, there wasn't one here. Despite all the beauty, I couldn't lose sight of the fact that if I came here, there would be no marching or exciting football games or standing in the middle of a field and blasting out solos with a whole backup band behind me. Ever again. In my entire life.

I put my mulling aside as we arrived at the gates of the school, at the top of a hill at the end of Main Street (seriously, it was called Main Street). We drove up and down the three narrow roads that made up the entirety of the Covington College campus.

If the town of Covington was a movie set, than the campus itself was pure, unapologetic stereotype.

The buildings were dark red brick, half-covered in ivy, with leaded-glass windows that reflected the late afternoon sun. A small stream wound through budding trees and flowering shrubberies, with adorable little wooden bridges arching over it every so often. Dad rolled the windows down and we could hear the clear bell of a clock tower marking the quarter hour. The lawns were a delicate, dewy green, and students hurried around on neatly kept gravel paths in spring jackets and brightly colored scarves, heavy-looking backpacks and messenger bags slung over their shoulders.

I studied their faces as carefully as I could from a moving vehicle, and noticed that most of them looked … content. A good portion were even smiling, like they couldn't believe their good luck to be exactly where they were, among this loveliness, going to this school.

And, despite myself, I started smiling, too.

Then, with a sudden shock, I realized that they were all girls. I mean, I knew that it was an all-girls school, but it hadn't really sunk in until I looked across a busy path and didn't see a single person of the male persuasion anywhere.

"Oh, Ellie," whispered Mom dramatically, "I can see you fitting right in here."

"Yeah, maybe," I said vaguely, watching a girl walk along a path next to the car. She had light brown hair and a wide face like me, and she had earphones in and was holding two thick books. For a second, I envisioned my face over the strange girl's, seeing myself in her place, walking through this campus, belonging here.

Was it really possible?

Dad pulled into a parking lot beside one of the larger buildings. A sign indicated it was the administration building.

"Here we are!" he said excitedly, unbuckling his seat belt and throwing open the door. "Just in time for our tour appointment and maybe we'll be able to peek in a class, too! Let's go!"

It was the most exclamation points I'd heard my dad use in one speech since the last anti-war rally we'd attended as a fun family outing.

So we piled out of the car (some of us more reluctantly than others) and at that moment, my cell phone beeped. I pulled it out of my bag and saw that it was a text message from Connor.

> HOW GOES IT? PARENTS HAPPY NOW? ☺ MISS
> YOU.

I wanted to reply, but I wasn't sure what to tell him, and Mom was beckoning me toward the building. Dad had already disappeared inside.

"Come on, don't want to be late!" she said.

I slipped the cell phone back in my bag and walked up the broad stairs, feeling a bit like twenty-pound weights were attached to my ankles. I couldn't figure out why I should be freaking out, though … birds were twittering in the trees, and a cool breeze seemed to push me up toward the front door. Mom companionably linked her arm through mine, and I put on a smile for her.

We checked in at the front desk and were told that our tour guide, who was a current student, would meet us out on the front steps in a few minutes.

"She's one of our best," the receptionist said.

"I wouldn't expect anything less from a Covington woman," my mom told her mock-seriously, leaning on the counter. She then launched into a story about how she had graduated from here, and what things were like back in those days, and blah blah blah. The receptionist just smiled and nodded, having no doubt heard variations of this same story from a thousand proud mothers bringing their eye-rolling, high-school-aged daughters in for college tours. I admired her ability to keep smiling.

But it was a little more than I could handle at that moment, so I escaped outside. I sat down at the bottom of the concrete steps, took deep breaths and tried to decide exactly what I was feeling.

If I chose, this could be the place I would be next year—this could be my beautiful, ivy-covered school. I would be walking those paths. Carrying books. Drowning in words and ideas. Making friends with new people.

With a dim ache in my side, I thought of all those miles between here and where I'd come from, between Connor and myself. Between me and State and Kristen and Jake. How could I even consider coming here? How could I "pros and cons" *this* one out? How could I ever, ever—

At that moment, a low voice broke my unhappy reverie.

"Hey, are you Ellie Snow?" the voice asked, and I turned around and looked.

I nodded slowly, instantly intimidated.

The unknown girl's dark blue eyes gleamed, her wide mouth grinned, the reddish highlights in her short dark hair caught the light of the afternoon sun. She stood there with her hands on her narrow hips, wearing close fitting jeans and a bright purple T-shirt marked with the name of an indie rock band.

She was unselfconsciously cooler-looking than any girl

could even pretend to be back in the entire state of Michigan, let alone Winslow.

"Sweet. Well, welcome to Covington. I'm Alex Campbell and I'll be trying to convince you to come here next year. Sound good?"

And that, incidentally, was approximately the precise moment the *real* trouble began.

Five

eah, sure," I replied, casually, as if cool people asked me such questions every day. "Sounds good."

She smiled, and I was actually glad when my parents came tromping down the front steps. I took the opportunity to turn away and give myself a stern lecture.

Stop freaking out, I snapped at certain distracted parts of my brain that were wondering if Alex would be my friend if I came here. *You have a boyfriend back home.* Who is cute and who you love. You have a plan. Also, you're not coming here anyway so you'll never see this girl again so FORGET ABOUT IT.

But I couldn't stop watching Alex, watching as she politely shook hands with my parents, took my mom's the-old-alma-mater crap with a good-natured grin. She was either really good at acting around parents or actually... really nice.

I didn't know whether to be giddy or relieved that there wasn't anyone else on the tour. This way, I'd have more of a chance to talk to her, but on the other hand, I'd have more a chance to talk to her.

"So, Alex, what's your major?" asked my dad as we walked across the campus. I cringed. That sounded so much like a pick-up line or something.

Alex didn't seem to find it strange, though. "Philosophy," she replied.

"Hmm," said my dad. "What exactly does one do with a philosophy degree?"

"Dad," I said, embarrassed. I couldn't believe he was questioning the educational objectives of a girl we'd just met.

But Alex just laughed, a sweet sort of chuckle that sounded genuine. And was it my imagination, or did she subtly wink at me?

"You have a lot in common with my parents on that topic," she said. "But don't worry, Mr. Snow, I'm planning on law school after this."

Oh, *great.* I knew what was coming then.

"Law school!" Dad boomed happily, like he had been searching his whole life for another lawyer and hadn't found one anywhere in the world until this moment. "Excellent plan. What field were you thinking of going into?"

Alex and Dad moved ahead of my mom and I, talking

law. Mom took the opportunity to nudge me and whisper "See? There are nice people here!"

"Shut up," I hissed back, my cheeks burning, hoping that Alex wouldn't turn around.

"Well, there are," she whispered. It was obvious Mom wasn't going to let this go until I acknowledged she was right.

"Okay fine," I replied softly. "You're right. Can we talk about something else?"

"Like how beautiful this campus is?" she said in a normal voice.

Alex looked back at us. "I'm glad you brought that up, Mrs. Snow. Let me tell you a bit about the history of Covington."

And as we walked around the lovely campus, Alex talked. And she talked. And then she talked some more. Normally, I'd be tempted to hate anyone who so clearly enjoyed the sound of her own voice, but I kind of enjoyed the sound of her voice, too.

Alex spoke so … confidently.

Although she was just a year older than me and didn't appear much older than anyone I currently went to school with (including my boyfriend, who happened to be very mature-looking for fifteen), Alex talked like someone much more experienced. Someone with facts, and practice discussing said facts, and knowledge to back her up instead of just dumb teenage bravado.

Suddenly, the fact that I was dating a guy who was

a sophomore in high school made my stomach clench in embarrassment, as it hadn't clenched in several months. It somehow had stopped really mattering. Until now.

"And that is why every third brick in the library archway is painted white," Alex finished up with a grin. Even though I hadn't been completely listening to every word, I still sort of wanted to give her a round of applause or something.

"Well, I never knew that when I was here," said Mom. "How interesting!"

We took a tour of the gorgeous wood-paneled library, and when Mom whisked Dad off to show him the place she'd always studied, I stayed behind with Alex.

"So, Ellie, tell me about yourself," Alex said with a friendly smile. One that seemed to say she was actually interested in hearing about me, not just being nice.

"Um, well," I said with a shrug, "there's not much to tell, really."

Don't tell her about band, don't tell her about band!

"Oh, come on," she said, nudging me a bit with her shoulder. "I'm sure all sorts of cool stuff happens back in Minnesota."

The fluttering stopped as if someone had stepped on a butterfly. With steel-toed work boots.

"Um," I said. "*Michigan.* I'm from Michigan."

"Sorry!" she said, clapping a hand to her forehead, looking genuinely embarrassed. And also kind of adorable. I'd always wished that I could look like that when I screwed up. "See, I'm from Seattle and, um, we sort of call that area the fly-over states. I mean, it's not meant to be offensive or anything."

"*Really,*" I said, offended.

You don't have to tell me that Michigan isn't the most exciting or interesting place on earth, but that was only for people who had at least *been* to, and preferably had *lived* in, Michigan to say.

"Is this what everyone's like here?" I continued. "I read something online about Covington being ridiculously snobby. I thought I'd give it a fair chance and see if I'd fit in, but maybe they're right."

Alex's eyes widened a bit, like she was actually upset about offending me. She backtracked. "Jeez, no. There are kids from everywhere who come here. I have friends from all over the country—and from Arkansas! And, like, the world. Seriously, Ellie from Michigan or Minnesota or Maine, I think you'd fit in just fine."

I turned away from her, the nervousness reinstated, afraid she'd see me start to glow. The idea that someone thought I'd fit in just fine—in these wood-paneled rooms, this lovely campus, this Other Place that was so very far from where I came from—made me irrationally happy.

"Anyway," said Alex, "we were talking about you. What do you do?"

"Um," I said, turning back toward her. "You know... stuff."

"Like what kinds of stuff?" Alex was looking down for some reason, a smile on her face.

I suddenly noticed that my foot was loudly tapping on the lovely marble floors, the sound echoing around the room, and stopped it.

"Stuff with things," I replied, shrugging casually. "Oh, there are my parents."

The tour complete, we left the library and walked toward one of the main classroom buildings.

"There should be a few classes still going on," Alex told us. "Though people don't normally like to schedule classes on Friday afternoons."

"Why?" asked my mom, who had apparently forgotten what it was like to be young. Though I had long suspected she'd always been a bit of a nerd. Which was completely different than being a band geek. At least *we* knew how to enjoy weekends, even if our idea of fun involved marching at football games.

"Well, because . . ." Alex trailed off and gave me a glance. Obviously she didn't want to encourage the idea of anything except studious, well-mannered behavior occurring on Covington's sacred grounds.

"Because that makes it hard to get a start on the weekend, duh," I said.

Both my parents pursed their lips. It's not like they could hold that against Covington. State had been ranked third biggest party school for something like a decade now.

"Is there a lot of drinking that goes on here nowadays?" my mom asked.

Alex seemed comfortable with this question. I imagined it was a common concern among worried helicopter parents who couldn't even imagine the possibility that their precious daughter had most likely already thrown up in someone's bushes at some high school kegger.

Not that I had ever done that. Seriously, I hadn't.

"Well, as you know, Mrs. Snow, there aren't many bars in town, and the ones on Main Street are incredibly careful about checking IDs," Alex said.

"Sure," said Mom. "Though back in my day, we didn't exactly need to go to the bars to find some beer, if you know what I mean."

Dad looked alarmed. "There's drinking...in the dorms?"

Oh, *Dad*.

Alex shrugged. "I suppose there is some alcohol around, but the RAs are pretty good about catching people. And no one likes to get in trouble."

She then cast a winning smile on both my parents. "We're all good girls here, Mr. and Mrs. Snow, I promise."

I snorted at her ridiculous earnestness, but managed to cover it up by pretending to cough.

"Besides," she continued. "It's not like there are any boys around to get in trouble with."

This seemed to comfort my mom somewhat. "That's true," she said, and laughed. "I remember the lengths we had to go to for dates back when I was here. Some girls would drive all the way to New York City just to meet boys!"

This threw me a little bit. I mean, it's not like I really enjoyed boys, as a group or in general. Connor and Jake were pretty much the only dudes in my age group that I didn't feel the constant urge to kick in the shins.

But to not have any people of the Y-chromosome persuasion around, ever? It was a weird concept that was just starting to sink in.

We entered a squat brick building that Alex told us held the largest number of classrooms on campus. We trailed her down a wide hallway and peeked into a small lecture hall where twenty or so students were paying rapt attention to a professor at a podium.

"Intro to Political Science," Alex told us in a low voice. "This, right here, is as big as classes get at Covington. Twenty-five, tops. The discussion sections are even smaller."

Mom gave me a meaningful look. We had already discussed how class sizes in intro-level courses at State often numbered in the hundreds. A lot of them had lectures broadcast online, so it wasn't even necessary to show up at class.

Not that I'd be taking many of those huge classes, seeing as I'd be in a lot of smaller music school courses. But if I ever wanted to branch out and study, say, political science, I'd just be one of hundreds.

"That's impressive," Dad was saying.

As we watched, one of the students raised her hand

to ask a question, and the professor stopped lecturing and called on her.

I laughed to myself at the mental image of anyone at State, in one of those 300-person amphitheaters, raising their hand in the middle of class. They'd probably just get ignored.

"So, what do you folks do for fun back at home?" Alex asked as we walked back toward the administration building.

"Well," said my dad, "just last weekend Ellie had a jazz band performance that was pretty good."

Alex turned toward me with a wide smile. "Jazz band?"

"Um … yeah," I said, trying not to anxiously search her face for signs of disapproval.

"Oh, Ellie is a wonderful musician," my mom chimed in, helpfully. "She was section leader in marching band this year. She had a solo and everything."

"Anyway," I said, quickly, "let's talk about something el—"

"What do you play?" Alex asked. "Flute?"

Anxiety swiftly gave way to irritation. Flute always seemed the Default Girl Instrument for anyone unfamiliar with band. "Uh, no," I said, shortly. "Not that there's anything wrong with flute, but no."

"Ellie plays trumpet," Dad said proudly. "She's very talented."

"Yeah, you already said that," I said. Why were they all of a sudden so excited about my musical pursuits?

A smirk was playing around the corners of Alex's mouth, like she knew exactly what was going on in my head and was enjoying watching me squirm. My hands began to tingle a little bit, like they always did when I was preparing for a confrontation.

"Trumpet, eh?" Alex said. "That's pretty sweet."

I'd opened my mouth for some snappy retort, but she caught me off-guard. *Sweet?*

"Really?" I said, not able to help myself.

No one had ever really thought that me being in band was all that interesting. I mean, my friends who were already in band didn't find it so special, and generally, non-band people were confused and even prejudiced about the whole premise.

"Oh, totally," she said. "I'm, like, the most unmusical person in the world. I love listening to music, but when it comes to playing I'm completely useless. I'm always in awe of people who can create their own."

Mom gave me a solid nudge with her elbow, which I was pretty sure would leave a bruise on my rib cage. What, she was some big band fan now that Alex thought it was impressive?

"Um ... thanks," I said, my cheeks warm. "That's ... nice of you."

I felt my phone vibrate in my messenger bag, and knew that it was Connor. Again. I decided to ignore it.

Six

My mom whisked my dad off for some sort of gross romantic dinner at a restaurant out in the countryside, and I was scheduled to stay with Alex for dinner in her dorm dining hall so I could get more of a taste of college life.

Frankly, I had been abjectly dreading the idea of hanging out with some stranger in some strange town for that many hours, but after the tour, I was pretty much convinced Alex was the coolest person I'd ever met and I didn't mind at all. I sort of wanted to study her in her natural habitat, to try and understand how someone could be so self-confident and happy, glean whatever I could because maybe I could be That Way someday.

"Yeah, the food sucks," she told me as we stood in line

for dinner. "But you'll get used to it." She guided me to a two-person table at the edge of the room, stopping at a few tables along the way to say hi to friends and quickly introduce me.

Alex seemed to know everyone in the entire room. And not in an annoying, social queen-bee way, but in a genuinely interested, nice way. I was beginning to realize she actually … *liked people.* In general, they seemed to delight her. Which was kind of a weird concept for me to grasp.

That didn't stop her from giving me some snarky asides about how that girl still gets care packages from her parents every week, or how that girl keeps all her sweaters in vacuum-sealed plastic bags because she is deathly afraid of moths, or how that girl is almost failing out of school yet still got trashed and threw up all over the communal bathroom last weekend.

"Some people have a hard time with leaving home," she told me, thoughtfully chewing a french fry. "Honestly, I don't think everyone is meant to go straight from high school to college. I don't think everyone can handle it."

Christ, what if she meant *me?* What if she was trying to tell me something?

"How do you know?" I asked, pretending to be interested in a piece of wilted iceberg lettuce. "If you're ready, I mean?"

"I don't mean *you*, if that's what you're wondering,"

she said, grinning. "I'm not sure if I've ever met someone who more needs to leave home than you."

"Thanks?" I said, not sure if that was meant as a compliment.

In response, she threw a french fry at my head. In a friendly way. "Chill out, Ellie," she said. "You take everything too seriously."

I couldn't suppress a smile. Though it totally reminded me of something that Connor would say.

Oh, shit. Connor.

I'd send him a text message later or something...

After dinner, Alex showed me her dorm room.

When I went on the tour at State, I'd briefly seen a dorm room but didn't have a chance to really examine it. Then again, it was basically a cinder-block room with two cheap-looking bunk beds—there wasn't that much to examine. So I was curious to see what I'd be in for, dorm-wise, if I came to Covington.

"I lucked out and managed to get a single," Alex said. "It's not much, but it works."

She opened her door with a flourish.

The room was beautiful, and Alex obviously had put a lot into decorating it. It wasn't that large—definitely smaller than my room at home—but she had covered up the plain white walls with pretty tapestries and scarves and framed, black-and-white photographs. Her bed had a silky blue comforter on it and at least five fluffy pillows. The dying sunset glowed through the green curtains, giving the room a kind of underwater feel.

I walked around, examining Alex's stuff, while she was in the bathroom down the hall.

Everything was sort of neatly cluttered: a pile of new hardcover books by her very fancy computer; her iPhone, which she'd just plugged in to charge; her closet bulging with clothes; and dozens of shoes scattered around on the floor.

It was pretty obvious that Alex's family had some money.

I looked closer at the pictures on the walls. They were clearly all by the same photographer and featured shadowed and faceless people in various stages of undress, long limbs stretched in ways that made it look like they were dancing.

I don't know anything about photography, but I knew these were beautiful. In, you know, a way that was kind of beyond my ability to explain or comprehend.

"Wow," I said, quietly.

"You like?" Alex said, from behind me.

I jumped at her voice, and we both laughed.

"Yeah, I do," I said.

I glanced over at her desk and saw a big, serious-looking camera sitting next to her computer and put two and two together.

"*You* took these?" I asked, staring at her.

"Yep," she said happily. "And I developed them myself. It's my little side hobby."

"Hobby? Wow," I said again. "That's amazing!"

I turned away for a moment so she wouldn't see me cringe at myself. Jeez, I sounded like such a little suck-up. *OMG Alex U R cool!*

She didn't seem to notice, though. She just beamed at me.

"Thanks, that means a lot," she said. "My mom's a photographer out in Seattle, actually, so it's sort of one of those things where I feel like I'll never measure up. And my dad just thinks it's ridiculous that I'm even spending time on it. He's the one who wants me to go to law school."

"Oh, whatever," I said, rolling my eyes. "You're obviously awesome at photography, no matter what your parents say. You should totally do it as a career."

She gave me a bashful smile, looking up at me from under lowered eyelashes like Princess Diana. "Thanks, Ellie."

"No problem," I said, and started biting my lip.

"You know, Covington has a couple of photography electives, if you think it's something you might be interested in."

"Um, I don't think I could do that," I said. "I'm pretty much just a band geek. My brain doesn't work that way."

"Sure you can do it!" she said. "They teach you everything. And I'd definitely help."

I had a brief vision of Alex and myself in some red-lit

darkroom, pinning photos up on a line like they do in movies.

"Well ... maybe," I said, and she grinned and nudged me with her shoulder.

We hung around for a while longer talking about classes, and then Alex suggested that we go hang out with her friends in their dorm room.

"They're awesome," she said. "You'll love them."

"Okay." I was suddenly nervous again. "Are you sure that—"

"It'll be a blast," she promised.

I called and left a message for my parents, telling them I was going to stay a little later.

There were two missed calls from Connor on my phone, but I ignored them. There just wasn't time to call him back.

"So you're sure you're cool with this?" Alex asked as we stood outside her friends' dorm room. There was a white board with a couple of silly drawings and some inside-joke handwritten messages, plus some pictures of famous actresses torn out of magazines.

"Sure," I said, with a shrug. I marveled at my own ability to act. Maybe Covington had a theater program, too.

"Liz and Becca are awesome," Alex said as she knocked on the door. "You'll love them."

The door opened, and a pixieish blond girl squealed "Alexiffic! My darling!" And then promptly launched herself into Alex's arms as if they hadn't seen each other in three months at least. I suddenly felt very uncomfortable. And stupid.

"Lizzy-bell!" Alex said with equal enthusiasm. The blond girl was very pretty, with smooth porcelain skin and long, thin limbs. I felt very gawky and chunky and unexceptional.

Liz beamed up at Alex, and then saw me standing awkwardly in the hallway.

"Who's this?" she asked, smiling brightly at me.

"This," said Alex, "is Ellie. She's a prospective from my tour this afternoon and she's hanging out with me tonight to get an idea of the real Covington experience."

"*Oh*," said Liz with a slight smirk, all sorts of meaning imbued in that one single word.

"Don't worry, she's cool," said Alex, shooting me a smile. I smiled back instinctually, trying to appear at ease and unbothered. What had I gotten myself into? Why had I agreed to this? I could have been safely back in the hotel room, watching TV and texting Connor!

"I'm sure she is, if you invited her," Liz said, and then smiled at me. "Come on in, guys."

She opened the door wider and a few minutes later I was sitting on a ragged futon, trying not to stare around the room too obviously.

It was a little grungy, and definitely not as nicely decorated as Alex's room, but it was cozy and comfortable and through the leaded-glass windows I could see the town of Covington twinkling below.

Alex sat next to me. She talked about classes with Liz and her roommate, Becca, a girl with curly dark hair and pink flower tattoos on both her bare feet. Becca had given me the same sort of up-and-down look and then apparently dismissed me.

My phone buzzed in my bag. I imagined Connor sitting there, staring at his phone, waiting for me. So while the other three were talking, I pulled out my phone and punched in a quick message.

Going good. Seems like a cool place.

I knew the total lack of any details would frustrate him, and indeed, he replied right away.

Yay! Want to hear more. Can I call?

It was kind of strangely irritating. Didn't he have any life of his own? I sat there, staring at the little screen on my phone and mulling. Then Alex turned to me.

"Everything cool?"

I pushed my phone back into my bag and smiled at her.

"Yeah, totally," I said.

"Good," she said.

Over by the window, Liz was struggling with something.

"Alex," she called in a whiny voice. "Can you help

me with this stupid vodka bottle? Becca screwed it on too tight."

Vodka?

"Sure." Alex jumped up and took it out of Liz's hands, easily unscrewing it.

Then, suddenly, all three of them were looking at me.

"Uh, you're cool, right?" Liz asked.

"Definitely," I said.

"You wouldn't, like, go blab to your parents or anything," said Becca, an edge to her voice as she pulled a glass bottle of orange juice out of the mini-fridge. "That would be pretty lame."

"Course Ellie wouldn't," said Alex confidently, which warmed me right up. She grabbed a few coffee mugs off the top of the microwave. Four of them. One for each of us.

I'd had wine often enough, at home with my parents. If they were having a glass with dinner, they'd pour me some too and it was no big deal. And there had been that time Kristen and I had stolen a bottle of Peach Schnapps from her parents' cabinet at 2:00 AM and shared it back and forth until we both felt woozy and had to go to sleep.

And, yes, I know that lots of people my age drink at parties and stuff. I just … um … hadn't been invited to anywhere in which that sort of thing occurred. And dating a sophomore, it wasn't like the opportunities had really increased all that much with senior year.

The point is, I wasn't a stranger to alcohol. I was certainly familiar with the concept.

But this unsupervised vodka-in-a-dorm-room thing? It threw me a little. I mean, that was kind of serious in a way I couldn't really put my finger on ... like the idea of having my own credit card or paying taxes.

It just felt more grown-up than wine at dinner and stolen Schnapps.

What if I got drunk? What if I said something stupid to these girls who I wanted to like me? What if my parents figured it out and were, like, disappointed? The opportunities for something to go wrong were endless.

Fortunately, I knew how to act like I was keeping it together. Even if my insides wanted to dramatically fly apart.

Alex turned and winked at me. "No worries, I'll mix you a weak one."

And the very small, almost negligible competitive part of me (ha) rolled over, woke up and stretched.

"Weak one?" I found myself saying. "No way. I can handle anything you guys can handle."

Alex's eyes widened appreciatively and she poured an extra measure of vodka into my mug.

"Go Ellie," she said. "I didn't know band geeks were so into the sauce."

I rolled my eyes. "Whatevs, dude. You obviously haven't known many band geeks."

What was I *talking about?!* Shut up, Ellie!

"Hand it over," I said, beckoning for the mug, my heart banging away in my chest. I held the rim up to my mouth and I could practically feel the alcohol fumes hitting my eyes.

And then, because all three of them were watching me, I took a huge gulp of vodka and orange juice.

For a few seconds, I was pretty sure I had been poisoned. Clearly, Liz had slipped pure acid into the mug while I wasn't looking—I was currently experiencing the complete and sudden decomposition of my throat. I put a hand up to my neck, half-expecting to feel a hole burned through the skin at the collar of my shirt.

And then the moment passed, and I felt the warmth spread down my insides. And then, weirdly, right up into my brain, where it sort of felt like it sat down and started a campfire.

I smiled brightly at the three of them and smacked my lips. "Tasty," I pronounced.

They all looked at each other with looks like *Well, all right then.*

As I sat sipping that first drink, the night began to seem much...easier.

I suddenly couldn't believe how hilarious everyone was...how smart the jokes were that Liz and Becca and Alex made. God, they were so smart! No one back in Winslow talked about things like this except for the 4.0 nerds, and they were so boring they'd never do anything fun like drink screwdrivers and discuss the juxtaposition of Lindsay Lohan and feminism and the increased incidences of women wearing leggings.

I didn't say much ... I didn't want to say anything stupid. As I sipped at my drink, even my own laughter at their jokes became sort of grating to my ears, but I still tried to soak in everything I could.

My phone rang in my pocket and I blearily pulled it out.

"Oh Christ, not him again," I said as I pushed the button that sent Connor's call directly to voicemail. It took me a moment to realize I had said it out loud, and that the other three were looking at me.

"Not who?" asked Becca with a conspiratorial smile.

I glanced around and they all looked amused. I hadn't mentioned the fact I had a boyfriend.

"Um ... " was all I managed.

"Some cute little high school boy?" Becca continued, in a sing-song voice. I sort of wanted to pinch her. Particularly because Connor was, like, two feet taller than her.

"He's not little," I muttered.

"Oh?" said Alex. "A big one, huh?"

"So he *is* your boyfriend," said Becca, like it was a fact that needed to be set down in stone.

And then I looked at the three of them, these girls who might be my friends next year, who I really wanted to like me, who seemed infinitely more at ease with themselves than I was even if it was fake ...

And I flat-out lied like a dog.

"No," I said, rolling my eyes. "Just some guy who keeps

following me around. Can I have another one of these vodka thingies?"

I didn't even feel guilty. Well, not then, at least. Alex got up to fill my cup again.

"Oh, I remember high school boys," said Liz with a mournful shake of her head. "God, was that ever torture."

"Some of them were cute," said Becca. "I had a few nice boyfriends."

"And how did that go for you?" asked Alex with a laugh. "Nice and easy?"

Becca smiled with something that looked like embarrassment. "Well...no, of course not. But my high school wasn't exactly the place to come out, believe me."

Come out?

"And you didn't have any cute Lizs to date, either," said Liz, ruffling a hand in Becca's hair.

And then it struck me. They weren't just roommates, they were... *together!*

Not that I had any problem with that or anything. I mean, there were guys and girls at Winslow who were openly gay. They sort of made up their own clique, in fact, with their LGBT club and all. They were made fun of about as much as anyone else, perhaps even less than band geeks as a whole were, and it wasn't something I had really thought about. They didn't, like, walk down the halls holding hands or anything.

But this was different. This was somehow real.

Alex was watching me like she knew what was going on in my head.

And I had liquid courage.

"So at Covington are there a lot of, um…" I trailed off, totally unsure how to phrase it without offending anyone and/or looking like a jackass.

"Lesbians?" supplied Alex.

I felt myself blush. "Yeah."

Liz and Becca both chuckled, like I was some silly little cute thing that had no idea how silly and cute I was.

"Yes, we're *everywhere*," said Becca mock-ominously. "Corrupting innocent young minds and bringing them over to the dark side!"

Liz gave her a playful shove. "Shut up, you'll scare her." She turned to me. "There are a fair number, probably more than at most co-ed schools. But then, Covington is all girls, so it's not a surprise that there are a higher percentage of lesbians. I mean, statistically."

I nodded. This made sense.

"Of course, lots of people are just trying it out," Alex said.

Liz rolled her eyes. "Right, well, why shouldn't they?"

I could sense this was a long-standing piece of contention between them.

"Oh, I'm not saying that they shouldn't," Alex said. "It's just a little bit… contrived and obnoxious. But then people trying to find their identities always are kind of contrived and obnoxious, I guess."

"So...you're not a, um..." I trailed off again.

"Lesbian," supplied Alex with a laugh. "No. *I* don't believe in labels."

"Speaking of trendy," said Liz, with a dramatic eye-roll.

"I don't understand," I said.

"Oh, here we go," said Becca, sighing. "Get ready for the lecture."

"Whatever, guys, it's not complicated," Alex said. "I just think people shouldn't have to put labels on who they love. And I don't think anyone should have to define themselves by who they love. I think that's just society trying to put us in boxes and tell us who we are."

I'd never heard anyone say such things. My mouth was probably hanging open.

"That means Alex doesn't want to decide between boys and girls," Becca explained. "Kind of annoying."

"Why is that annoying?" Alex asked, looking irritated, her blue eyes flashing. "Why can't I just like people in general?"

"Because no one knows what to expect from you," Liz muttered, in a way that indicated she didn't really want a response.

"Anyway," broke in Becca, "Ellie, tell us about your boy."

"Oh..." I said. "He's really nice."

Really nice and won't freakin' stop calling me, I thought as my phone buzzed again with an ignored voicemail.

"And?" Liz prompted.

There was not a single cell in my body that wanted to

tell these cool, self-confident girls I was dating a sophomore.

"He's nice, and … um … "

"Where did you meet?" asked Becca. "That's always
an easy question."

Uh, not really. Not in this case.

"Band," I said, quietly. "Marching band."

"Really?" Becca asked. "I always wondered what that
was about. We didn't have a marching band at my school.
Do you really just take instruments out on a football field
and play as you walk around?"

"Um, more or less," I said, the vodka turning over in
my stomach. Liz and Becca shared a glance and giggled. It
made me feel approximately two inches tall.

"I think it's cool," said Alex decisively, as if the matter were settled. "I sure as hell couldn't do that, so major
props to anyone who can."

"Though you know, Ellie … there isn't a marching
band at Covington," Liz said in a slightly condescending
tone, as if she thought she were helping.

"Yeah, I know," I semi-snapped back. "Thanks."

"There's other stuff, though," said Becca. "Like …
uh … aren't Jamie and Maya in a jazz band or something?"

"Ellie's in jazz band!" Alex interjected excitedly. I
looked sharply at her, surprised she remembered that small
fact from earlier in the day.

"Yeah, so there you go," said Liz. "When you come
here you can still play … what is it that you play? Flute?"

I managed not to burst into a fireball on the spot. *"Trumpet."*

"Dude, awesome!" said Becca. "That's so tomboyish of you!"

Leave it to the lesbians to be the first non-band girls to think that me playing the trumpet was awesome.

A few minutes later, it was time to leave. Becca was yawning and Liz had laid her head down on Becca's shoulder.

"Maybe we should take off?" I suggested to Alex. The vodka must have seeped into my eyelids and voice-box; it was making me feel mature and mysterious.

"Yeah, I guess so," Alex said. "I still need to walk you back to the hotel."

I stood up decisively. "Nice to meet you guys. Thanks for the drinks and all."

"No problem," Liz said, waking up enough to smile at me. "Good luck with your decision."

Alex gave me a light hip check. "Oh, Ellie knows what she's going to do," she said. "Right? Ellie?"

I nodded slowly, then said, "I do?"

She rolled his eyes. "Of course. You're coming here and you're going to hang out with us."

Liz and Becca both nodded at me like this were obvious.

"Seriously, Ellie, don't go to some big state school," Liz said. "You'll just get lost. That's what all my friends back in Maryland have said." She looked at Becca, raising her eyebrows as if encouraging her to say something, anything.

"Um, right," Becca said dutifully. "Plus, you're probably too smart for State. It'll just make you dumber."

I felt my eyebrows involuntarily furrow. Jake and Kristen weren't the most academically oriented people that I knew. Kristen had barely made it into State, in fact, which I would never in a million years bring up to these girls. But I wouldn't call Jake or Kristen dumb. They just had different priorities, skills other than the academic ones that had always come fairly naturally to me.

"Hmm," I said noncommittally, not meeting their eyes and trying not to show how bothered I was.

"Once you get here and settle in, you'll forget all about home," said Becca with confidence. "And when you go back, it'll seem strange and small and ugly, like a piece of someone else's past."

Alex chuckled. "Please forgive Becca," she said. "She's going through a literary phase."

I chuckled too, but her words rang somewhere deep within me. Did I *want* to forget about home? Did I *want* Kristen and Jake and most of all Connor to become pieces of someone else's past?

As if in answer, my phone vibrated in my pocket once more. If he had left another damn voicemail…

"Hey, let's take a shot of vodka before we go," said Alex. She directed Liz to pour straight liquor into our coffee mugs, and we stood around in a circle.

"To Ellie," Alex said. "May she make the right choice."

We clinked our glasses and, watching them out of the corner of my eye, I imitated the way they threw back the vodka and then somehow managed not to gag at the choking taste and the feeling of liquid fire. People drank straight vodka for *fun*?

The warmth in my stomach became hotter as the taste melted away, and now it felt like a furnace had been lit in my mid-section. I looked down, half-expecting to see a giant sweat-circle on the front of my T-shirt.

"Shall we go?" asked Alex, her face looking a little shinier and more high-colored than it had a moment ago.

"Yeah," I said.

The hallway was raucous and full of people. We stumbled through, Alex's hand on my back steering me through the groups of girls. I staggered a few times and was grateful for the help.

Seven

Out on the front steps of the dorm, there had to be at least twenty girls and a few guys sitting around in small groups, gesturing with cigarettes and talking animatedly. A low cloud of smoke hung over them, and I tried not to breathe in too deeply.

And then we were past them, into the fresh night air, walking along the path that lead down to town and my parents' hotel. Lamps glowed orange every twenty feet, and crickets chirped loudly on the unseen lawn.

After the closeness of the closet-like dorm room, and all the loud music and talking, to be out in the quiet night was exhilarating. Especially as the alcohol in my stomach continued seeping into my brain.

"Is it always this cold here?" I asked, wrapping my arms around myself.

"Allow me, madam," Alex said, taking off her jacket and draping it over my shoulders. She grinned at me, and I gave her a light hip check that she seemed to lean into. We were walking so near each other that our arms were never not touching.

My phone vibrated in my pocket with the unheard voicemails. The crickets seemed to be chirping louder.

"So, Ellie Snow, will I be seeing you here next year?" Her words were light, but there was an edge, almost a dare to her tone of voice.

"I don't know." I sighed deeply. "I don't know what to do."

"I think you probably should just come here. Because otherwise I'd have to drive to Michigan and beat you up."

Then, with vodka-infused courage, I looked over and smiled at Alex. It felt strange, foreign, halfway insane to be having a half-flirty, half-jokingly-hostile conversation like this with another girl. A girl who seemed to speak my language, even more than Kristen.

"Oh yeah? That's interesting. Because the chances of you being able to kick my ass are just laughably small. I have, like, twenty pounds on you."

She smirked at that, and then reached over to pat me on the shoulder. "Right, little girl, just keep telling yourself that."

I felt a surge of competitive excitement stir in my

stomach. "Hey, I like to tell myself the truth, dude, that's all."

"Well, maybe you should give it a try now," Alex suggested. Energy curled in my fingertips. "But first … " She trailed off.

"First what?" I said.

"First you'll have to catch me."

And with that she took off into the dark at the side of the path, then into the blackness beyond. I could hear the sound of her feet hitting the damp grass in the distance.

I stood there for a moment.

She was tall and had a runner's body. My sprinting abilities were somewhat limited. My phone vibrated yet again with the unanswered messages, and the crickets took it up a full notch.

I really didn't have to consider what to do. I took off after her.

The cool night air whipped around my face. The trees were vague shadows and it was so dark I felt like I could be flying, like I was eight years old again out on the summer night streets in front of my house, playing tag with the neighborhood kids. I held on to the collar of Alex's borrowed jacket with my hands and let it billow out behind me like a superhero's cape.

There was no chance of actually finding her—she could be anywhere. So after running a hundred feet or so I stopped and stood still, looking up at the clear sky and the thousands of stars glimmering overhead.

Some sixth sense made me look to the right, and I saw Alex's shadow right before she slammed into me and sent us both sprawling across the ground. She laughed and rolled next to me, half her body still on top of mine. I felt dew from the grass seep into the back of my shirt; I had lost her coat along the way.

"Hey, jackass!" I said. "I thought you were supposed to be showing me a good time, not tackling me!"

"Hmm, silly me," she said from the darkness. I could feel the vibrations of her voice through her back, smashed against my chest. "I thought I *was* showing you a good time."

I couldn't help but giggle. "Yeah, I guess so."

"Weirdo," she said.

"Freak," I replied.

She exhaled loudly and I felt her tensing to get up. I felt acutely that it was a moment for decisive action—it was as if the scale could be tipped to a point where something like this would never happen again, if I just lay there and allowed her to get up.

"Wait," I said, "don't get up. These stars are awesome."

"Yeah, they always are here," she replied, settling back down. "So much better than in the city."

She shifted all the way off me and we lay in companionable silence, our arms still overlapping.

"Well, tell me about this boy," she finally said. "Some band geek, huh?"

"Um, yeah," I said, and laughed morosely. "Duh."

"What's his name?"

"Connor. He's a sophomore." The words fell out of my mouth before I even considered them.

"In *high school?*" Alex got up on one elbow. "You've got to be kidding me."

I stayed silent, cursing the truth-serum vodka. It was exactly the reaction I'd been expecting from her. And I was pretty sure I knew what was coming next. Some Psych 101 analysis of how I was afraid to grow up, that obviously I was immature and scared, saddling myself with a fifteen-year-old when I should be looking ahead to adulthood. Maybe even judgments about the legality of the situation.

"You know," said Alex, and I closed my eyes, bracing myself for the inevitable judgment. "I've never met someone like you before."

Which was not what I was expecting.

"Um, in a good way?" I said, hopefully, opening my eyes again.

"I'm not sure," she said, sounding uncertain. It might have been the first time I heard her sound genuinely confused.

I stayed silent, trying to talk myself out of getting up and flouncing off in a huff. *Not sure?*

"You just seem kind of…angry underneath," she said. "And, like, smart and driven and that whole marching band thing and whatever, but sort of a control freak. Like, you're dating some guy who's so much younger than you so you can boss him around? And then being all prickly about everything? And I don't get why. Your parents seem cool, your life seems okay. Why all the anger?"

I sat up, my heart pounding. "Alex, you've known me for approximately eight hours."

"I'm good at reading people."

"Well, you're not good at reading *me*," I said, even though she had pretty much summed me up better than anyone else ever had. "And you don't know what you're talking about."

She was silent for a moment, and then her shadow shrugged. "All right. If you say so."

I hugged my knees to my chest. "Do I really seem angry?"

Alex reached up and rubbed my back, strong fingers kneading at the knots under my shoulder blades. It almost felt like she was reaching past my skin and directly into my muscles, rubbing each fiber.

For a moment I tensed, surprised; then I relaxed into her fingers.

"Sort of," she said.

I sighed, trying not to think about the fact that a girl was touching me. A girl had never touched me like that. Kristen and I hugged, or whatever, but not like this.

"I'm just really freaked out," I said, softly. "I don't know what to do with my life, and I hate that."

"I know how it is," she said soothingly, her hand still on my back, now moving up to my neck. "I was totally there a couple of years ago."

"And I thought I had figured it out, but then I came here and it sounds corny but it's like a whole new world," I continued. "But choosing this path eliminates the other path, just as choosing the other path and going to State would make this become nothing. They are... what's the phrase? Mutually exclusive. And I can't even stand the idea of deciding."

"Which is why you were planning on just going to State and doing the same thing you've always done."

"I... suppose." It was kind of painful to admit.

"Well, what if you don't do the same thing you always do?" she said, casually. "What if you branch out?"

"And that would somehow solve all my problems?"

"What *are* all your problems?" she asked. "Maybe it just seems like you have problems because you're in the same place you've always been and you're about to go do the same thing you've always done. Marching band. Same friends. Whatever. Ellie, it's just boredom. You're meant for more."

I opened my mouth to retort, to tell Alex she had it all wrong, but nothing came out. Because it actually made sense.

She took her hand away and I missed it instantly.

"Do you think *this* is really more?" I asked, quietly, spreading my hands out to indicate the Covington campus, despite the fact she couldn't really see me.

"I can't tell you what to do with your life," she replied, even though it seemed like that had been exactly what she was doing. "But if Covington and some big state school right by where you grew up are your two options, then yes—I'd say this is more."

"Snob," I muttered, lying back down on the ground.

"What?"

"I said, you're a freakin' snob."

"Well, maybe I'm a snob," she said from the darkness, nudging me with her arm. "But I also just know you can do better on all accounts. I mean, a fifteen-year-old? Seriously?"

My phone buzzed in my pocket and suddenly I noticed the stars were starting to swirl. "Yeah, I know." I sighed. "Also, I think I'm really drunk."

Alex laughed. "Come on then, let's get you back to the hotel," she said.

"Okay," I replied meekly, holding on to the grass as if it would stop me from being flung off the face of the earth and into the quick-moving sky.

Alex got up and offered me her hand. "Come on, crazy girl."

I grabbed onto her dew-dampened fingers and Alex pulled me to my feet, after which I stumbled clumsily into her arms. She held on to me for a long second before letting go.

Eight

My mom woke me up the next morning in the hotel room with some unnecessarily loud packing. When she saw me glaring at her from under the covers, she stopped.

"Well, you were certainly out late last night," she said. "What time did you come in?"

I blinked at her, and then buried myself back under the blanket.

"Dunno," I mumbled.

Actually, I did know. It had been 2:00 AM and the fact she hadn't heard me come in was, quite frankly, amazing. I hadn't been very graceful.

Mom came over and threw the cover back.

"Were you with that nice Alex girl?" she asked with

barely contained excitement. "She was so nice. Your father thought she was nice too. Just a really nice girl."

"Is she also nice?" I mumbled, curling my knees up to my chest on the blanketless bed and shutting my eyes.

There was a long moment of silence.

"Are we going to be able to trust you going away to college?" Mom asked. "Are you ready to be responsible for yourself?"

Mom always did this. Bring up Serious and Weighty Issues at, like, the worst possible times. Such as on the morning I was nursing what I was pretty sure was my first hangover. And when I refused to discuss the Serious and Weighty Issues, she'd get all mad, like she was about to do in 3, 2, 1...

"*Elaine*, are you even listening to me? Get out of bed right *now!*"

I sighed and sat up. My head thumped a little on the edges of my vision, but otherwise I seemed to be all right. I stretched my arms out in front of me and noticed the grass stains on my elbows at the same moment my mom did.

"What's that from?" She grabbed my arm and twisted it around to get a better look.

"Mom, ow!" I said, ripping my wrist out of her grasp. "Jeez! It's nothing, leave me alone."

"Ellie, why do you have grass stains on you? Did you ... fall on the grass?"

"I don't know," I answered primly. "And I have to take a shower. Where's Dad?"

"He went to grab a paper," she said. "And then we're meeting him for breakfast. Why do you smell like smoke?"

She wasn't going to trick me into replying. I gathered up my clothes and went into the bathroom. It took a solid five minutes of scrubbing to eliminate the physical evidence of last night's insanity.

I sort of wished I could reach in and scrub my brain, too. And then reach back in time and scrub the past.

What had I done? What had I admitted to that strange and unknown girl in my drunken stupor? She probably thought I was an idiot. She probably thought I was worse than an idiot. I had babbled at her about being ashamed of my sophomore boyfriend, and my anger issues and God knows what else, and . . .

As I picked at my waffles at the restaurant Mom swore was the best breakfast joint in town, I tried to not feel like a complete jackass for as long as possible, but eventually failed miserably.

What had I done?

I still hadn't responded to Connor's calls or text messages. He probably thought I was dead. Or worse, he probably thought I'd ended up making out with some other boy, which is what had happened last fall when we were first getting together.

But I felt like what actually happened was even more a

betrayal than that, even more disloyal. I had bad-mouthed him, I had been … attracted to someone else in a way I never really had been to him.

What?

I excused myself and went to the restaurant bathroom to look in the mirror.

My hazel eyes stared back, appearing the same. The grass stains on my elbows were gone. When I thought of Alex, something stirred in my midsection. Something that had sort of gone dormant whenever I thought about Connor lately.

I mean, I adored Connor, of course. He could make me laugh even when I was in the darkest mood. He had the most gorgeous blue eyes I'd ever seen. He was smart and sweet and had made me feel a sort of special that I'd never felt before in my entire life.

But exciting? Not terribly, anymore. I liked kissing him at every available opportunity, the sensation of his long arms wrapped around me, smelling his minty shampoo and all that. It had just started to feel kind of safe and routine.

Especially compared to Alex.

I'd been drunk, though, right?

I realized what I was thinking, the ways in which I was trying to justify my unjustifiable actions, and a wave of disgust hit me. Was I really that obnoxious girl who got bored with nice boyfriends because they were too … nice? How gross and cliché.

"You kind of suck," I told my reflection.

When we went to check out of the hotel, Alex was waiting in the lobby.

My parents beamed at her like she was the second coming or something. I, on the other hand, felt a little bit like I had been punched in the stomach. I hadn't been expecting to see her again.

Or at least not this soon.

"Thanks for showing Ellie college life," my mom said, like I'd been locked in a dungeon for years and had no idea what college entailed. "And for giving us such a great tour yesterday."

"No problem, Mr. and Mrs. Snow," said Alex, who had easily slipped back into her Respectable Young Woman mode. "It's been a pleasure."

We stood there awkwardly for a moment, and then Alex turned toward me.

"Ellie, can I talk to you for a minute?" She winked at my dad. "Last minute recruiting pitch."

He chuckled and said, "We'll grab your bags, Ellie. Take as long as you need."

When they were out of sight, Alex took my hand and pulled me outside and around the corner from the front door. She leaned against the brick wall and we looked at each other.

She was dressed in a fleece jacket, jeans that were torn

at the knees, and bright pink Converse sneakers. I was shocked by how much I sort of wanted to touch her.

"What are you doing here?" I said. Inexplicable annoyance bubbled inside of me, though I couldn't really figure out why. It's not like what I'd said last night was her fault.

"I just wanted to make sure you were all right."

"All right?" I said. "Why wouldn't I be?"

"You just seemed sort of freaked out last night, and I felt bad—"

"You're just covering your ass, right?" I said, part of me cringing at how hostile I sounded. "Making sure I don't report you for corrupting the people you're supposed to just give tours to?"

She looked genuinely alarmed for a moment. "Um..."

I managed a very fake-sounding laugh. "Just joking, dude, no worries."

"No worries?"

I shrugged. "Yeah, no big deal. It was just...you know ... whatever."

She was searching my face, biting her lip. "Right...just whatever."

"But, um, thanks for showing me around and all. It was educational."

"Educational," she said, looking off somewhere over my left shoulder as if trying to work that through her head.

"You can stop repeating everything I say," I told her.

Alex sighed. "Look, I just wanted to say sorry, that I didn't plan on, um, *that* happening and I feel bad about it.

It's not like that ends up happening on every tour I give or anything. You're just sort of ... my type."

"Why should you feel bad?" I asked, skipping over the last part of what she'd just said. "It was just fun or something, right?"

"True," she said.

There was a long pause. I studied my feet. Her *type?*

"I didn't scare you away, right?" she asked softly. "It would be really cool if you came here next year."

"I don't know," I said.

"Can I email you?" she asked. "I mean, if you don't come here, and ... I just think we're meant to be friends."

"Maybe," I said. This was very strange. Why did she even like me so much? She was at least twenty or thirty times cooler than me. I was just some freaked-out high school band geek, and she was some brilliant photographer/philosopher/future lawyer. Why would I even matter?

"Well, here's my contact info," she said, handing me a torn piece of notebook paper. It had her email address and Instant Messenger screen name on it. "I guess just ... well, it's up to you, Ellie."

"Okay," I said, because I didn't know what else to say.

Before I knew what was happening, Alex leaned forward, put her arms around me, and hugged me tightly. After a second of trying to control my breathing, I relaxed and hugged her back.

She smelled like cinnamon.

"Follow your heart," she said quietly. Then she put her

lips on my cheek. Not, like, a kiss. Just resting there without moving.

After a few moments, I tensed and pulled back.

"I should go find my parents," I said. I walked away, leaving her leaning against the wall. I could feel her eyes on me until I turned the corner.

I flipped open my phone in the car to find eight unread text messages and five new voicemails. I sighed and leaned my head back against the seat, considering my options, and decided to take a nap instead of dealing with the inevitable.

When I woke up, my parents wanted to have another State of Ellie's College Decision discussion in which Nothing Was Resolved. Then we stopped for sandwiches and listened to an NPR program about lab rats, and with one thing and another, it wasn't until we were an hour from Winslow that I ran out of excuses to keep avoiding my phone.

I looked at the text messages first. There was one from Jake and one from Kristen, just checking in to ask how things were going.

But the remainder of the text messages and all of the voicemails were from Connor. The first few texts were cheery and casual.

Going good?

Then,

Hope ur having fun. Miss you Love you.

Then they started getting a little alarmed—and then panicky—and then resigned. The series culminated in a voicemail Connor left at 2:00 AM, approximately three hours later than he normally goes to bed (though, I suppose, technically it was spring break). His voice was desperate and exhausted, as if he had just gone through a deathbed vigil that hadn't ended well.

"Ellie, please call me back... I'm really worried and, um, I don't know why you're ignoring me. I mean, I don't know if you're ignoring me or if your phone just ran out of battery or, um, you just forgot or something but call me? Okay? Love you. And..." he trailed off, as if considering what he was about to say. "I hope that you're not... I mean, hope to talk to you soon."

I knew exactly what that "I hope you're not" meant. I hope that you didn't manage to find some college guy at an all-girls school and start making out with him.

There was one last text message from him, sent this morning. I could almost see the despondency in the pixels on the screen.

Hope ur alive.

I sighed loudly, causing my mom to turn around and look at me.

"Are you okay?"

I shrugged. "I guess. It's just … "

"Just what?" Mom looked a little over-eager, ready to be let in on the gossip.

"Nothing." I ignored her until she turned back around.

There was only one way I could respond to Connor, and that was with false cheeriness.

> HEY YOU! JUST GOT YOUR MESSAGES … THINGS BEEN BUSY. ALMOST HOME. TALK TO YOU SOON.

Connor was waiting in the driveway when we pulled up.

Nine

I got out of the car and walked up to Connor. His face was inscrutable, and since he generally walked around with an open expression somewhere between contentment and abject joy, I knew this was a problem.

"Hey there," I said, as my parents walked around us and into the house. I hoped my own face was equally unreadable. Or at least not completely guilty.

He bit his lip and looked down at the ground. I reached over to touch him, but he leaned away from me.

Uh oh.

"Did you have your phone turned off or something?" he asked. "Did you seriously not get any of my messages until an hour ago?"

"Oh, right…listen, I'm really sorry about that but things got kind of crazy and—"

"I was really worried," he interrupted. He almost looked teary. "You could have at least—"

Now I interrupted him. "I said that I was sorry, Connor. And I was visiting a college…it's not like I had all sorts of time to reply to messages. Especially not when I got, like, twenty-five of them. Was that really necessary?"

"I was worried," he repeated in a small voice. I hated it when he got like this, all little-boyish and whiney. Why couldn't he just attempt to act like a grown-up?

Because he's not even sixteen years old yet.

I reached out and grabbed onto his arm, not allowing him to get away this time.

"I'm sorry," I said. "Okay? I'm sorry that you were worried."

"What were you doing?" he asked.

I shrugged and then I lied. "It was just an exhausting trip."

"Are you going to go to Covington now?"

Translation: Are you going to leave me here?

Maybe he should have been a little more worried about that before. "I don't know," I said. "I have to think about it."

"Did you…meet people?"

"A few. They were cool."

"Cool," he said. "I see."

Annoyance began to grow inside me, but it lost the

fight against guilt. I snuggled up to Connor's chest, even as he stood there as unmoving as a stone statue.

"I'm back now, though," I said. "Aren't you glad to see me?"

Tentatively, almost reluctantly, I felt his arms move and go around me.

"Yes, I'm very glad you're back," he said, resting his chin on top of my head.

It felt…good. It felt familiar and warm and like home.

And compared to where I had just been, it also felt dull and painfully ordinary.

I leaned back and looked up at him, and he looked down. On my tiptoes, I kissed him full on the mouth, unabashedly. Even though we were out in the front yard where my parents and all the neighbors and passing cars could see.

He was stiff and still for a moment, but then he warmed up and began to kiss me back. His arms twisted around me more tightly, his fingers kneading into me like he needed to prove to himself that I was really there, his breath quickening in my mouth.

We broke apart, both of us panting.

"Wow, what was that for?" he asked, a smile playing around the corners of his lips as if he couldn't help himself.

I shrugged and slipped my hands into the back pockets of his jeans, pulling his lower half toward me. "Oh, you know. I missed you."

He leaned down and put his mouth on my neck. "Did you really?" he asked softly.

"Of course I did," I said, arching my neck to give him more access. He began kissing me again, distracted, as I knew he would. As I hoped he would. I needed him to forget. *I* needed to forget.

I heard the living room window slide open and a discrete sort of cough come from inside. I knew my parents had seen us making out in the front yard.

"I should go in," I said softly, my eyes closed. "I need to unpack and stuff."

"Okay. When can I see you again?"

I gasped as he bit down gently on the skin halfway between my ear and the edge of my shoulder. I needed Connor close to me. I needed to be close to him. More than anything, ever, I knew this fact.

And not just because I needed to prove that I still wanted to be with him. I swear.

"Tonight," I whispered. "We should both sneak out."

"The park?"

"Yeah," I said. We could be outside, on the grass, just like with Alex. That would erase it all. "At midnight."

His lean body moved against mine and all I could smell was him.

When I went inside, Mom looked up from her book and gave me a pursed-lipped look of disapproval.

"Ellie, you know you're going to hurt that boy when you leave," she said. "Why are you getting so entangled? Don't you want to be free?"

I looked at her levelly. "Mom, I love him. I've told you that."

She rolled her eyes. "Love? Really? Don't you think that—"

"If you say I'm too young to be in love," I interrupted, "I am going to scream."

Her face softened a bit. "You're not too young, Ellie, but *he* is. If we were talking about a college guy, this would be a different conversation."

"What do you mean?"

"We'd be talking about birth control," she said, shrugging. "And how to protect yourself."

Sometimes my mom actually showed hints of real coolness, especially for someone who was starting to receive AARP magazines and was within spitting distance of retirement. Or at least she sometimes showed amazing practicality. I mean, Kristen's mom would probably sooner lock Kristen up in a chastity belt than discuss safe sex.

Little did she know that Kristen and Jake were *totally* planning on doing it on prom night. That's what Kristen said, anyway. Personally, I thought it was a little cliché, but she was so excited that I didn't want to say anything mean about it.

But still, even if it seemed cool on the surface, I resented Mom's implication that I couldn't be privy to some sort of important knowledge just because of a small factor like my boyfriend's age.

"And we're not talking about safe sex because Connor's a sophomore?" I asked.

"Duh," she said. I cringed. I hated it when she tried to talk young.

"That makes all sorts of sense, Mom," I said. "We've been dating for months now. Get over it."

"Ellie." She got up and walked over to me, putting her hand on my shoulder. "He's too young. You're moving on to college. Let him go . . . it'll be better for everyone."

"Wait a second," I said, shrugging her hand off. "When did this change from 'don't have sex' to 'break up with him'? I thought you'd stopped being ridiculous about this. He's my boyfriend. We're committed."

"When I saw how you two . . . what you were . . . I saw how you kiss," she said, looking uncomfortable. "I know that sort of kissing. I've been there. I just want you to be careful."

"I thought you liked him!" I said, exasperated. Even as I sort of wanted to hear about how she'd been there. Even if 'there' had occurred over thirty years ago.

"I do like him," she said. "Connor is a very nice boy. But the operative word here is *boy*. And you're almost an adult, Ellie, and with that comes responsibility. You're the one with more power in your relationship, and you need to realize that and be the grown-up."

"Ugh," I sighed. "I'm so done with this conversation."

I was done with it because I had already begun to feel like she might be right. Not that I'd in a million years admit that to her or to myself…

No! I wanted Connor! I loved him! I had figured out the answer and the answer was Connor!

"Just think about what I said," Mom told me. "Do what you know is right."

I snuck out that night anyway.

Ten

And that is how it came to be that I ended up creeping across dark, damp grass for the second time in as many nights, on my way to do something crazy and probably regrettable.

Just like at Covington, the crickets were chirping with abandon and the stars felt like wee spotlights, looking down at my human silliness. The dew on the ground crept over my flip-flops, and the skin between my big toe and my next biggest toe started to rub raw in the damp.

I could only see the outlines of the trees near the spot Connor and I had made our own since the week we met. We'd even come here over the winter, building a snowman on the spot where we'd first gotten to know each other.

"Connor," I whispered, irrationally not wanting to

speak aloud even though we were hundreds of feet from any of the houses, which were all dark anyway. "Are you here?"

There was no answer. Just crickets. Always those damn crickets.

Great. He probably had gotten caught by Mr. Barr on his way out of the house and was now grounded and wouldn't be able to go to prom and—

Familiar arms grabbed me around my middle. He pulled me back against his body, his breath warm in my hair.

"Um, hi," I said, laughing quietly.

"Hey," Connor said back. His hands began roaming down my sides, then up under my shirt. "So, this is kind of cool."

"I know," I said, my breath coming more quickly. "Why didn't we do it before?"

He spun me around and pulled me up toward his face and we kissed. In the dark, with no one watching, no one knowing where we were, it was crazy and exciting. Like kissing someone I'd never kissed before.

Which you VERY recently thought might be better than this, my snarky conscience reminded me.

I pushed aside all doubts and kissed Connor as hard as he was kissing me. It almost became a little competitive, a bit like a battle, who could kiss the most enthusiastically. I took control by pulling him down on the ground, pushing him back against the grass, leaning over him.

"Ellie," he gasped between kisses, "I've never seen you like this before. What's going on?"

It was true—I never had *felt* like this before. I almost always let Connor take charge when we made out. Even if I kissed him first, I'd let him set the pace; I'd let him try and push it farther and test the boundaries. He was the guy, after all . . . I figured that was sort of his place.

But I was feeling wild, my head was chaotic. I had to prove something, but I didn't even know what that something was and my brain and body were whirling. I wanted Connor, right? I wanted to make him gasp, feel him lose control, show myself that he was the one who could make my body happy, the one I needed.

"Shut up," I replied, attacking his neck. "Also, you can't see me. It's dark."

He groaned softly as I pulled his shirt up. When he tried to reach up and put his hands in my hair, I pushed his arms back down on the ground, holding tightly to his wrists.

"Whoa, boy," I said. "I'm in charge here."

He groaned again, but didn't say anything. I moved to lay my head against the light hair on his chest, resting my cheek against his ribs so I could hear his heart beating wildly under my ear.

This was the person I loved. I wanted to show him that. Erase any doubt in my mind or his that I loved him and would do anything to make him happy.

And down, down, down I kissed over the soft skin of his belly. To the buttons on his jeans, which I fumbled with in the dark. And then I kept kissing and didn't stop.

We walked toward my house a half hour later, silent. He had insisted on escorting me home, even though I didn't want him to do it.

"What if a cop drives by?" I whispered. "You'll get picked up for a curfew violation!"

"So will you if you're alone," he replied.

"No, dude," I said. "I'm eighteen. I'm legal."

This seemed to momentarily jar him.

"Oh … right."

I didn't want him there. I wanted to be alone, to think, to walk the orange-lit streets by myself and ponder what had just happened and how I felt about it. Which I couldn't figure out with him walking *right there*.

Connor had picked up on this.

"Are you okay?" he asked. He put an arm around my shoulder that I instantly wanted to shrug off. I didn't, though. That would have been too obvious.

"Yeah, I'm fine," I said.

He took his arm away on his own.

"You don't seem fine," he pointed out.

"I am," I said, shortly.

"Is it about what … um … just happened?" he asked.

Yes.

"I don't know," I said.

He was quiet for a moment.

"Do you want to talk about it?"

No.

"Um ... what's there to talk about?" I asked.

Connor seemed to be at a loss. I was, too. How do you talk about "it" without it being massively awkward?

Okay, and it wasn't "it" it. It was sort of the step before "it." According to some people. Other people said it was just as significant as "it" and had scary commercials of people with mouth herpes to back them up, but I wasn't sure about that.

At least I could be grateful that Connor was a bona fide virgin in every sense of the word.

"Look, dude," I said. "It's no big deal. Um ... I just got sort of carried away, I guess."

"Do you regret it or something?" he asked, much too quickly. "I mean, I didn't pressure you or anything, right?"

I snorted at that idea. "God, no."

"I mean, I wanted you to do it—"

"Really?" For some reason this sort of shocked me.

"Uh, every guy thinks about that, Ellie. Like, pretty much all the time."

I wrinkled my nose. "Weird."

"Well ... I don't want it to be a one-way thing," he said. "I want to—"

"No," I cut him off. "We're not talking about that right now."

"All right," he said. He seemed to easily accept this.

We were only a few houses away from mine now.

"You can go back now," I said. "You have a long way to walk."

"Are you sure you're okay?"

"Yeah, go ahead." For some reason, just looking at him made me clam up, feel weird and kind of . . . gross.

We stood on the sidewalk. He looked at me. I looked through him.

"Ellie," Connor said, taking my face in his hands. "I love you. You know that, right?"

I nodded instead of saying anything, willing myself to look him in the eye.

He seemed to be at a loss about what to say next.

"I'm not sure what's going on," he said, finally. "You coming home from Covington and being all . . . you know."

"I'm not really sure what's up, either," I admitted after a moment, letting my head fall to the side, my cheek resting in his hand. "Can we talk about it later?"

He nodded.

"I love you too," I said quickly, throwing my arms around his neck. I kissed him quickly on the cheek, and then turned and took off lightly toward my house. I didn't look behind me until I was at my front door. By then, he was out of sight.

Eleven

$\mathcal{I}$ got up the next day and didn't know what to do with myself. So I called Kristen. She and Jake had gotten home from Florida the night before.

"Oh my God," she said. "I want to hear everything about Covington and most of all why you're not going there."

I laughed. It took a lot of effort.

"All right. Coffee?"

"Be there in ten."

It wasn't long, then, before we were sitting across from each other at a table at Espresso Café.

We talked first about their trip to Florida. It had involved a lot of time on the beach and many slow, romantic walks with Jake. I tried to look interested, but I was too wrapped up in my own head to keep it up for long.

"You look … different," Kristen observed.

My heart pounded in my chest. "Really? Weird."

"What happened out there?"

"Out where?" How did she know about the park? "Oh, you mean at Covington?"

"Um, yeah."

"Oh, you know," I said, shrugging. "Just a college visit or whatever. I met some people, had a tour, the whole deal."

"Right," she said, aggressively stirring her hot chocolate. "Met some people."

"Are you mad?" I asked.

"Should I be?"

"I don't think so," I said, confused.

Kristen mulled this over for a moment.

"Well, did you meet people cooler than me?" she asked with an awkward laugh, not looking me in the eye. And I realized what this was all about—that Kristen, like Connor, was afraid I was going to up and leave her. That I was important to her and she didn't want to lose me to another world.

And just like with Connor, I felt a rush of guilt, knowing that I was seriously thinking of doing just that. Be lost to another world, I mean.

"Of course not, Kris," I said, like that was the silliest thing ever. "They were a bunch of bitchy snobs, just like I expected."

And I fit right in.

Kristen looked relieved. "Really? You're sure?"

"Totally," I said.

"Okay, good, because we both need to send in our housing packets and I want to talk about who's going to bring a TV for our dorm room."

And with that, she was off, back to the agreed-upon plan of going to State, rooming together, being in band.

Having everything be the same for four more years...

I nodded at the right places, told her I'd check into the appropriate things. Eventually, she realized I wasn't entirely with her.

"So, tell me more about these bitchy snobs," she said casually. "Who did you hang out with?"

"Mostly my tour guide, Alex, and then with some with her friends," I told her. "Alex was actually really cool. She's a philosophy major and is going to be a lawyer, but she's also a photographer and takes these amazing pictures. But she's somehow also really nice and ... what?" I'd noticed Kristen looking at me with wide eyes and a strange sort of smile.

"Um," she said. "You're talking about this girl like she's some guy you have a destructive crush on. Like you talked about Nathan freshman year before he humiliated you."

"Whatever," I said, shrugging it off even though my heart was pounding. Was it really that obvious?

"Yeah," said Kristen with a laugh. "Did they turn you

into a lesbian in just a few hours? I've heard lots of stuff about those all-girls schools."

This annoyed me. "No," I said. "There aren't that many more gay people than at any other school." I gave her the line about it just being more obvious because it was all women, that people were more comfortable experimenting, et cetera.

"Sure, right," Kristen said, rolling her eyes. "You're just more comfortable with this Alex, then?"

"Are you some sort of homophobe?" I found myself spitting at her. "What's your problem?"

"I don't have a problem," she said, unfazed, "but you do. And his name is Connor."

"Connor isn't a problem," I said loftily. "He's my boyfriend and we're just fine, thanks."

"Did you know he called me?" Kristen asked. "On Friday night, when you wouldn't answer your phone. He thought that maybe I'd heard from you."

"Ugh, stalker," I muttered. "He didn't leave me alone that whole night."

"Ellie, he was just worried about you," Kristen said. "Why didn't you pick up your phone? Does it have something to do with this Alex girl?"

"No, of course it doesn't," I snapped back.

"Okay, fine," she said, backing off. Kristen was well aware of my limits, and we both knew I was reaching one with her.

We both stared moodily out the window for a moment. Then I took a deep breath, remembering what Alex had suggested about the fact I'm not actually angry, just bored. That what I really needed was to make a complete life switch.

And that was not Kristen's fault, and I shouldn't take it out on her.

"Look, Kris, I'm sorry," I said. "I'm just confused and freaked out and I don't know what I'm doing. But I didn't have to be a bitch to you."

She looked surprised at this change in my attitude.

"It's okay, I'm used to it," she mumbled. "And also, what do you have to be confused about? I thought you said you weren't considering Covington."

Be honest, I heard Alex's voice say in my head. Be true to yourself.

"I am," I said. "Considering it, I mean. I think it might be good for me."

"Oh." She nodded and bit her lip. "I see."

"But if I went there, I'd still come back and everything," I said quickly, rushing to assure her. "We'd still be friends and talk on IM and all the same stuff we do now except…"

"Except you won't actually be around," she pointed out. "You'd leave us behind."

"It's not *behind!*" I insisted. "You're moving on to a new stage of life, too, you know. Everything will be different anyway. You and Jake probably wouldn't even miss me."

"Don't tell me what I won't miss." Suddenly Kristen's hostility was back and she looked as fluffed up and claws-out as an angry kitten, though I knew she'd much prefer to be more intimidating.

"Okay okay, I won't," I said. "Jeez."

We sat in silence for another minute.

"So are you going to hate me forever now?" I asked. "Just for being confused?"

Kristen exhaled loudly. "No, I suppose not. I just wish you'd stick with the plan. I mean, what about band? Are you ready to just give up band?"

"That's what I've been doing since middle school," I said. "Sticking with the plan and being in band. Is it really so terrible to consider doing something else?"

Kristen looked at me, unblinkingly.

"How much of something else? Am I even going to recognize you when you come back?"

"Um, yeah," I said. "I'll still be me."

"Right," she sighed. "You were there for just one night and you already sound like a stranger."

Yeah, maybe that's a good thing.

Twelve

*L*ate that night, I sat at the desk in my room, staring at my computer screen. There was a picture of Connor and me on my desktop, taken when we'd celebrated our seven-month anniversary. He'd given me a stuffed lion playing a trumpet. I don't even know where you can buy such a specialized stuffed animal like that... it must have taken him a long time to find.

I sighed and opened my IM client to see what everyone was up to. Kristen and Jake were both away. Connor had been idle for a half hour and was probably doing homework or hanging out with his cousins or avoiding me because I was crazy.

The rest of the friends on my buddy list were just casual acquaintances, who I didn't IM unless there was a real reason. I felt kind of lonely.

"You should be practicing," I said out loud to myself, glancing wearily at my trumpet on its stand in the corner of the room. Technically, I was still supposed to be auditioning for that music education scholarship to State. I should still be keeping my options open.

But trumpet seemed so boring and ordinary all of a sudden. Just like State.

I opened up the packet of Covington stuff, even though I'd read every brochure twenty times at least. The slip of paper that Alex had given me with her contact information fell out.

I considered it for exactly two seconds, and then typed her name into my buddy list.

She was online!

It took about five minutes for me to figure out what to say in my opening instant message. Would "hey there" sound too intimate? Would "what up" sound too idiotic?

Then I realized, this was just a girl who was a friend who I was messaging. Nothing more. What would I say to Kristen?

TRUMPETGRRL: HEY! IT'S ELLIE.

I watched the screen anxiously, biting my index finger like it was a food source. She didn't reply immediately ... she must have been away from her computer. Or else she closed out the window as soon as she saw me and was considering putting my screen name on a block list so I could never IM her again.

I tooled around on Facebook for a while, unwilling to completely give up, and just as I was about to sign off in embarrassment and go practice, the instant message window started blinking.

> Karma3012: Hi Ellie! Sry I was in the hall talking to people.

The wave of relief that passed over me was probably visible. I was giddy. She had replied!

> TrumpetGrrl: No prob. Just wanted to say thanks again.
> Karma3012: Of course! How was the drive back?
> TrumpetGrrl: Looooong.
> Karma3012: ☺

We talked about casual things for a while—what my parents thought of the tour, what we had each done the rest of the weekend.

> Karma3012: Liz and Bex thought you were v. cool.
> TrumpetGrrl: Yeah, they were really nice.

KARMA3012: THEY SAID THE NEXT TIME WE ALL
  HANG OUT WE SHOULD DO JELLO SHOTS.

The next time? They weren't just being nice, they actually
wanted there to be a next time? And they cared enough
about some random potential new freshman to even plan
out the drinks menu for that next time?

So. Awesome.

TRUMPETGRRL: HAHA THAT SOUNDS LIKE
  TROUBLE.
KARMA3012: PROBABLY! SO HOW WAS SEEING
  YOUR BOY TOY AGAIN?

I probably would have gotten pissed if anyone else except
Alex had called Connor my boy toy. But she, it seemed,
could say just about anything and I wouldn't be pissed.

TRUMPETGRRL: HE WAS MAD THAT I DIDN'T
  CALL HIM WHILE I WAS GONE.
KARMA3012: HMM ... A LITTLE BIT CLINGY?
  MEBBE KIND OF POSSESSIVE?
TRUMPETGRRL: HE'S NEVER REALLY BEEN LIKE
  THAT BEFORE ... I THINK HE'S JUST FREAKED
  OUT.
KARMA3012: WELL HE'S SCARED OF LOSING YOU.
  I DON'T BLAME HIM.

Did that mean what I thought it meant?

We talked for hours after that, long after my parents had stopped by my door to say good night and suggest that I turn in, long after the time I normally forced myself into bed in order to get enough sleep to function.

My other friends came and went online. I talked to Kristen and Connor about nothing; I was a terrible IM conversationalist since I was so wrapped up in my conversation with Alex. Connor seemed suspicious and wanted to get in some deep discussion about what had happened the night before, but I told him I was looking up online sources for my AP Euro term paper, and he left me alone.

It was like I could talk to Alex about anything and everything and she instantly got what I was trying to say. She figured out immediately that something big had gone down (ha) between Connor and me last night. And somehow it didn't feel weird to tell her exactly what happened.

KARMA3012: DUDE, DON'T FEEL GUILTY ABOUT THAT.

TRUMPETGRRL: REALLY? IT JUST SEEMS LIKE IT SHOULD BE KIND OF A BIG DEAL.

KARMA3012: TOTES NOT A BIG DEAL! EVERYONE DOES THAT. JUST MAKE SURE HE RECIPROCATES. ☺ ☺

And suddenly, even though I didn't particularly want to think about what reciprocation involved, I didn't feel guilty about what had happened. Alex told me not to be! *Everyone* does it!

Vaguely, in some much more rational part of my head than the part that was doing the talking, I realized that this was kind of ridiculous. I'd only known this girl for a few days and suddenly I was hanging on every word she said like she was my best friend. Like she actually knew me.

But she's not getting mad at you for just being yourself, the floaty, irrational part of my brain cooed. *She just wants you to be happy. She doesn't want anything out of you.*

Bullshit, rationality said. *Everyone wants something out of everyone. It's the way the world works.*

Finally it was after midnight, and I had to get to sleep.

KARMA3012: IT WAS SOOOO NICE TO TALK TO YOU ... SO GLAD YOU WEREN'T WEIRDED OUT BY YOUR VISIT.

KARMA3012: I KNOW THAT COVINGTON SEEMS LIKE KIND OF A STRANGE PLACE, BUT NOWHERE IS PERFECT ... AND I THINK YOU'D FIT IN.

TRUMPETGRRL: PROBABLY. BUT MY FRIENDS HERE ARE GOING TO KILL ME.

KARMA3012: YEAH THAT'S THE HARD PART. BUT THEY'LL MOVE ON TOO AND GET OVER IT. AND YOU ALREADY HAVE FRIENDS HERE, YANNO?

Yes, I did know.

TrumpetGrrl: Thnx.

Karma3012: Night night, sweetie.

Is it really terrible that I didn't think about Connor at all as I was drifting off to sleep?

Thirteen

*E*veryone was acting weird at school the next day, but I barely noticed.

Kristen was being kind of prissy and distant, apparently still upset by our conversation at Espresso Café. But how could I care about that when all I could think about was walking through Covington's lovely quad, eating in that dining hall, having those new friends?

In the band room before school started, Connor was odd and treated me like a particularly delicate doll, as if I had to be tiptoed around just because of what had happened on Saturday night. He kept asking me if I wanted to talk, looking worried that I might explode at him.

But I just brushed him off and thought about how cool it would be to live just down the hall from Alex, able to hang out and talk and drink vodka whenever the mood struck.

And not even having to deal with boys and the trouble they caused if I didn't really want to.

Jake was the only one who seemed unsurprised and normal.

"So you loved it there, hmm?" he said with a knowing look as we walked down the hall toward Bio. "Looks like I just might be right about something after all."

"Yeah, yeah," I said. "You were right. You're the smartest person in the entire world, Jake, and we're planning to throw you a parade."

He pulled my ponytail and I bumped him with my hip, our way of showing friendly affection.

"I'll miss you next year," he said.

I looked sharply at him, and he smiled. The smile was a bit grim around the edges, though.

"Well…I don't know if I'm going there for sure," I said slowly.

"Yeah you do," he replied. "You already see yourself there instead of State, don't you?"

"Sort of."

"Then what are you waiting for? Just do it. Decide."

"I…can't yet," I said.

"Is it Connor?" he asked.

"That's part of it," I said. "And you and Kris. And not knowing if I'm making the right choice, and a bunch of other stuff." I couldn't quite put my fear into words.

"Yeah, I get it," Jake said. "But do what's right for you, Ellie. Don't worry about what everyone else thinks."

Which sounded exactly like something Alex would say, and I suddenly wished she were here to talk to about all this.

Senior Prom, the end-of-high-school activity I was least looking forward to, was scheduled for that Saturday night. So it was necessary to smooth things over with Kristen. She and Jake and Connor and I were going in a group. We were planning on taking pictures over at Jake's house, and we had rented a limo for the drive to the hotel where prom was being held.

And that wouldn't exactly be very comfortable if Kristen continued not speaking to me.

"So we're going for our hair appointments at three on Saturday, right?" I asked her at lunch that day, plopping my bag down beside her. Sometimes the best solution is to act as if nothing is different.

She gave me a baleful sort of look, and then shrugged.

"Yeah, guess so," she said. "If you're still *planning* on going to prom."

Who doesn't like a little bit of passive-aggressiveness with their lunch?

"Kristen, of course I'm still planning on going," I responded as nicely as I could, with no visible eye roll. "Why wouldn't I be?"

"Oh, I don't know, maybe you're going to visit some of your new friends or something."

"Are you done now?" I asked. "Seriously?"

We had a brief staring contest, and then she blinked. I won.

"Yeah, I guess I'm done," she said with a sigh.

"Whatever happens next year, prom is going to be great," I said cheerfully. "We'll get our hair done and put on pretty dresses and get our pictures taken and go dancing and it'll be just lovely! I can't wait!"

She was grinning at me now, fully aware of how much bullshit I was shoveling. My dislike of dances was well known, but I had come around a bit since dating Connor. It was always a better time when you had a cute boy saying how nice you looked and asking you to dance.

"It'll be fun, Kris, I promise."

"Can I get that in writing?" she snarked.

And everything was back to normal with Kristen. For the moment, at least.

We had jazz band practice after school, so being around Connor was unavoidable. Just like in symphonic band, we sat directly next to each other. Except in jazz band, Connor was first chair and I was second.

I had to give the boy *something*. Jazz had never particularly been my thing, and he was better than me at improvising trumpet solos.

"Can we hang out after this?" he asked me softly while

Mr. Barr was working with the saxophone section. "I think we need to talk."

"Really, about what?" I asked innocently.

This seemed to confuse him. "You don't think we need to talk about Saturday?"

"What's there to talk about?" I said. "Everyone does that."

"They do?" he asked.

"Sure," I said. "Not a big deal."

His eyes widened and he leaned closer in to me, his lips almost touching my ear. This sort of thing usually would have made me melty, but today it sort of felt invasive of my personal space.

"So it might happen again?" he whispered.

God, boys really do have one-track minds.

"Maybe," I said, leaning away just as Mr. Barr suggested we might think about joining the rest of the group.

I drove Connor home, trying to make light conversation about prom, but he wasn't buying it. He sort of slumped in the passenger seat, looking every inch a petulant teenager.

"Dude, what's your problem?" I finally asked, after he heaved a big emo sigh instead of responding to my chatter.

"Nothing," he said.

"Yeah, right," I said. "Out with it."

He looked over at me with his beautiful blue eyes, blinked a few times, and repeated, "Nothing."

I pulled up in front of Mr. Barr's house and turned the car off. I looked over at him and raised my eyebrows.

"Fine," he said. "I just feel like you've been different ever since you came back from Covington."

"I just came back two days ago," I said. "What do you mean?"

"Well…" he appeared to be considering his words carefully. "I feel like I'm boring you, and like you don't really want to talk to me. And what happened on Saturday night was kind of weird, like you were trying to prove something."

I cringed. So it was *that* obvious?

"And now you don't want to talk about it," Connor continued. "And, I don't know, things seemed to be going really great but now they're not and…"

He seemed near tears. I always found this kind of irritating, to be honest.

"Connor, you told me I should go visit Covington," I said, trying to keep my voice soft and calm like I was talking to a scared animal. "Which was good advice. I liked it there, and it made me think about things. I don't really understand why you're so upset."

"I'm not upset that you went there, just that you seem different now," he said.

"I'm not different," I insisted.

"Whatever." He crossed his arms.

I sighed heavily. "I'm sorry if things seem weird. But can't we just have a good last couple of months living in the same town? Can't we have fun at prom and all that?"

He was silent for a moment. "I guess."

I leaned over, pulled his face toward mine, and kissed him. After a few seconds, he started kissing me back. And somehow it felt both as familiar as home and as boxed-in as a barbed-wire cage.

The kissing didn't really seem to make him feel better, and he still looked upset as he opened his door.

"Love you," I said as he got out of the car.

"You too," he said after a moment, and shut the door.

TrumpetGrrl: I don't know if I can make it through the summer here.

TrumpetGrrl: This place is driving me crazy...

Karma3012: Yeah I know the feeling... you'll survive.

Karma3012: I promise.

Fourteen

Any animosity that Kristen still held for me had vanished by prom day. She was in her element, and nothing would deter her from having the most fabulous prom *ever* in the whole history of proms.

Privately, I thought it was ridiculous how much she had hyped up what seemed like just another obligatory and awkward high school event. But I didn't see a point in telling her. It would only hurt her feelings.

Plus, I'd kind of enjoyed having my hair done up in an elaborate cascade of curls, even if it was practically shellacked to my head with hair spray. And my dark purple dress with the spaghetti straps was definitely the prettiest thing I'd ever owned (even if it required industrial strength undergarments to keep everything in place).

And Connor looked damn fine in a tux. That was for certain.

When he saw me, he gave me an odd sort of smile. "You're beautiful," he said. Like it was a fact not up for dispute. I smiled back at him.

"So are you."

We seemed to have come to an uneasy sort of peace over the past few days. The sort of peace where you know there are undercurrents of craziness and things bubbling right below the surface, but for now it was easiest to just ignore them. We hadn't really hung out much outside of school, me busy with studying and talking to Alex and Connor busy with whatever it is sophomore boys do.

Once the stress of prom was over, I'd promised myself, I'd try and figure things out with him. We would sit and talk until there wasn't anything left to talk about and everything would be explained and on the table.

And then things would be fine. But for now, it was all about prom.

Kristen was adorable in a frilly pink princess dress. Jake was rocking his tux as well, and the four of us together managed to look better than just a bunch of band geeks playing dress-up. We looked a little bit like … adults.

Even Connor.

Three sets of parents plus Mr. and Mrs. Barr stood around snapping pictures.

My mom gave me a hug. "I never thought I'd see the

day when you would willingly get dolled up to this extent," she said. "You look lovely."

The comment didn't even annoy me, though it probably should have.

I guess I never really thought I'd see the day, either.

In the midst of all the craziness and camera flashes, I barely had time to register that Connor was now acting a little strange and distant. He hadn't said more than a few words to me since the compliment, and his hand around my waist during the posed pictures felt kind of stiff and lifeless. Like he didn't particularly want to touch me.

I chalked it up to nerves, though, and ignored it.

The limo arrived and the four of us piled in, our parents waving us off. Kristen and I couldn't stop giggling and she had her camera out and was clicking away.

"Connor, get closer to Ellie and give her a big old kiss!" she urged.

He just sort of blinked at her for a minute, and then slowly moved toward me.

"Go on, kiss her!" Kristen said, her camera held up to her face.

I looked over at him, and his eyebrows were knitted together.

"What's wrong?" I asked, thinking that maybe he felt sick or something.

"Nothing," he said quickly. "Take the picture, Kristen."

He put his lips to my cheek and for the first time I could

remember, his breath actually felt cool on my skin. Like he had just been sucking on ice cubes.

I even shivered a little, involuntarily.

So I felt sort of subdued and couldn't quite work my way up to Kristen's level of excitement as we entered the ballroom at the downtown hotel. The theme of the prom was Flower Garden. (Has anyone ever adequately explained why proms even need themes? I mean, as far as I'm concerned, they should all be called the Uncomfortable Prom or something.) Some junior-year kids had spent hours making bright paper flowers and stringing them everywhere. Even I had to admit that the effect was pretty.

Kristen, of course, was in raptures over it. She made me take pictures of her and Jake against every available backdrop, including the punch bowl.

We sat down at our white-clothed table, which we were sharing with four other band seniors—including Brandy Jenkins, my least favorite person in band. We smiled fakely at each other across the table and complimented each other's dresses (though I personally would never have even considered a T-shirt in that shade of yellow, let alone an entire formal dress).

But, really, most everyone looked great. I started to re-catch a little bit of Kristen's enthusiasm, this feeling that we were really coming to the end of an era, that we had completed and accomplished something important, and that we deserved to celebrate while dressed up fancily.

As we ate dinner and gossiped about the people at the

surrounding tables, the only dark spot was Connor. He was sitting next to me like a gloomy little rain cloud, hardly participating in the conversation and barely looking up from his food.

I nudged him when everyone else was talking. "Are you okay?"

He shrugged, not even meeting my eye.

"Come on, what's wrong?" I said softly.

"I don't want to talk about it here," he said.

"When, then?"

"I don't know," he said. "Later, I guess."

I began to feel more than a little annoyed that he was being such a drama queen at my senior prom, even if I didn't care that much about prom itself. I mean, Connor was a sophomore and technically had two more of his own proms ahead of him, while this was my last chance to actually have a good time at one (unless I came back next year), and he was making it all about him.

So I ignored him until people started getting up to dance.

"Are you guys coming?" asked Kristen.

I looked at Connor, who was examining his cuff links.

"In a minute, I guess," I told her. "We'll meet you out there."

She shrugged and walked away.

When we were the only people left at our table, I turned to Connor.

"Are we going to at least dance?"

"I guess so," he said sullenly, as if it were a ridiculous idea to dance at Prom but he was willing to humor me.

I grabbed his hand, which strongly resembled a limp, dead fish, and pulled him out onto the floor.

We joined the group during a fast song, all of us in a tight circle. And even though I knew from past experience that Connor was fully capable of dancing well enough for a teenage guy, he just sort of stood there and shuffled back and forth, from foot to foot.

Abruptly, a slow song came on and people broke into couples. I turned to Connor and put my arms around his neck, vowing to make this appear as normal as possible even if he was being a jackass.

"Come on," I hissed. "Put your hands on my waist or something."

He obeyed but didn't say anything, just looked over my shoulder with a faraway expression, as if he wanted to be anywhere else but here.

My annoyance gave way to anger. This was all sorts of ridiculous.

"All right," I said, stepping back and throwing his hands off my hips. "Outside. Now."

I stalked through the swaying pairs of smiling, happy couples, hoping that the rage wasn't too apparent on my face. No need to let everyone know that my boyfriend was being a complete tool. Especially not when I knew my whole class probably thought it was amusing I was with a sophomore in the first place.

I stepped out into the corridor and looked behind me. Connor was taking his time walking through the tables, his shoulders slumped over and his face plainly miserable. He looked like he was being lead to the guillotine or something.

And that's when I felt the first thrill of very real fear. What was going on? Was this something more than just a run-of-the-mill misunderstanding?

I waited until he had followed me out of the ballroom door, and led him toward a secluded alcove where the pay phones were.

He leaned up against the wall and heaved a sigh as big as the world, as if he hadn't slept in days.

Come to think of it, he sort of looked like he hadn't slept in days.

"Okay, what's going on?" I asked, hands on my hips.

"I don't think this is the right place to talk about it," he said.

"I disagree," I said. "Whatever it is obviously can't wait, since whatever it is has obviously made you incapable of acting mature at my freakin' senior prom. Just spit it out and let's deal with it."

I cringed inwardly at the anger in my voice. He cringed outwardly.

"Okay," he said, after biting on his lip for a few seconds. "Okay, fine. If you really want to do this now, we can."

"Do *what?*"

"Ellie, I've been thinking," he said. "Ever since you came back you started acting weird, and now it seems like you already have one foot out the door to go to Covington..." he trailed off uncertainly.

"Yes?" I prodded.

"Well, after the way you acted last weekend in the park, I'm pretty sure you cheated on me out there somehow and—"

"What?" I burst out. "You think I cheated on you?"

"It's how you've been acting," he said softly. "I'm not stupid, you know."

My stomach tied itself in a neat little knot. So it really had been that obvious that something had happened. I thought I'd managed to hide it, pretend it away, but Connor had figured it out anyway.

But of course my first impulse was to defend myself by any means necessary.

"Do I need to remind you that Covington is an all-girls school?" I said.

"Yeah, I know that," he said. "I'm not an idiot. But I don't know... maybe there were guys around somehow or... something. It doesn't matter, and I don't really want to hear about it."

"I did not cheat on you," I said. *Well, not technically at least.*

"Well," he said, shrugging, "whatever. The point is that I realized you would do that to me again, and then when you sort of … jumped on me, I also realized something else. Which is that … " he paused, and then looked down at his feet. "I don't think I love you anymore."

I'd only lived for eighteen years, sure, but from that moment on, I knew I would always remember those words coming out of his mouth in exactly that order. The tone of his voice. The way he was standing there, slouched against the wall and not looking at me. The pale pink flowery wallpaper and the air conditioning vent that was blowing down on my nearly bare shoulders and giving me goose bumps.

And especially how the words couldn't have hurt me any more if each one had been an individual punch to my gut. Possibly even with brass knuckles. That had spikes.

"What?" I said, in a thin voice that didn't sound like my own. "You *what?*"

He took a deep breath, as if steeling himself, and looked me right in the eye. "I don't think I love you anymore."

There was that pain again in my midsection. I unthinkingly put a hand on my stomach.

"Why?" I found myself asking, as my vision became blurry with tears.

"I don't know. It just happened. Or unhappened. Or whatever."

He put a hand on my shoulder, one of his big familiar hands that I had held so often, felt around my shoulders and on my body and bare skin. A hand I had kissed and adored. But now it was the hand of someone who had just hurt me worse than anyone had before.

"I'm sorry, Ellie," he said. "You're really amazing and I'm sure you're going to do awesome stuff. But I just don't see any point in us being together anymore if I feel this way. I don't want to live a lie or anything."

"But I'm about to leave!" My voice was starting to sound shrill. "Why would you do this now? And at *prom!* I mean, who *does* that?"

"Shh, you're yelling," he said, looking around anxiously. "I didn't want to talk about it here, I told you that. But you insisted, so I'm telling you now."

I crossed my arms tightly across my mid-section as if I could hold in my heart, which I was sure was disintegrating into small pieces that would never be found.

Yes, I had experienced some mixed feelings about my relationship with Connor lately. Yes, I still wasn't able to think about what had happened with him last weekend in the park without feeling panicky and kind of gross. Yes, I had come to accept the fact we might not work out as a couple once I left for college.

But no one wants to hear that they're *not loved*, especially not from the one person who has ever said it in a romantic sense.

I looked up at Connor, acutely aware that my mascara was probably running down my cheeks in watery gray rivulets of ugliness.

I took a deep breath and he looked at me expectantly, a little fearfully.

"I can't believe how much of an asshole you are," I said, in what I hoped was a calm and measured tone. "And I can't believe how much of an idiot I was for expecting you to be mature."

He looked down at his feet again.

"You go around like you're something special, like you're better than other guys, like you're more sensitive and grown-up or something," I spat at him. "But you're not. It's all an act. You're just a scared little selfish boy, just like the rest of them."

I saw his forehead wrinkle, and I knew I had hit his weak spot. So I kept going. I felt a thousand angry words swirling in my throat, waiting to come out as weapons that I would insert directly in his brain. I wanted him to feel the same way I was feeling—dismissed and unwanted and unlovable.

"Giving you a chance was the biggest mistake I ever made," I said. "You're just a loser who flunked out of your last school, and I should have seen that from the start."

It's funny how coming up with the right comeback words at the right time, instead of two hours later when you're somewhere else, can actually make you feel worse.

Connor's face fell, and I could tell he was near tears too. My stomach twisted again, this time in regret. And for some reason, my mom's recent advice came into my head, about how as the older person I had a responsibility toward him.

A few tears rolled down his cheek, but he looked at me defiantly, as if daring me to say more.

But I felt dangerously close to bursting into dramatic tears myself, and realized there was nothing I wanted more than to be alone somewhere.

"See ya," I said, sweeping past him in my purple prom dress. I stopped and turned around. "I'll put all your crap in a box on my front porch. Feel free to have someone drive you by to pick it up."

I hoped more than anything that he couldn't see my shoulders shake with epic sobs as I walked away.

Fifteen

After spending ten minutes in a distant bathroom that I hoped no one from the prom would stumble upon, I snuck back into the ballroom to grab my purse from under my chair at the empty table. Everyone else was dancing and Connor was fortunately nowhere to be seen.

I called a cab from the hotel lobby. I hadn't bothered trying to find Kristen. I didn't want to ruin her night as well as mine, so I texted her.

WENT HOME EARLY. NO WORRIES. TALK TOMOR-
ROW.

I hoped she'd be so caught up with Jake and their planned Big Step Forward tonight that she wouldn't make an issue out of it.

The house was dark when the cab dropped me off. My parents had stopped caring about a curfew as my senior year drew to a close.

Part of me was glad I wouldn't have to do any explaining, but another part sort of wished I could go to their room and crawl into bed with them, like I did when I was five and afraid of thunderstorms. Like they could protect me.

I was on my own. Desperately, horribly alone with no one to talk to now that my boyfriend had dumped me.

So I did the only reasonable thing I could think of that didn't involve spray paint and rotten eggs—fired up my computer to un-friend Connor on Facebook and block his screen name on Instant Messenger. The last thing I wanted was to be reminded of his existence through online mediums.

I signed on, noted that his away message still read "At Prom," emphatically flipped off the screen, and promptly blocked him. It was almost freeing, as if making that mouse click made him un-exist.

Which it didn't, of course. Not really.

I sat and stared at the wall above my computer for a minute, wondering just what the hell I was going to do now.

And then an instant message window popped up on my screen. It was Alex.

I'd already told her all about the big night, how I ended up sort of looking forward to it. And she had been excited for me, or at least pretended to be, and asked for pictures. And now I'd have to explain to her what happened.

Oh well. Might as well get practice at telling the story.

KARMA3012: YOU'RE HOME EARLY? HOW DID IT GO?

TRUMPETGRRL: ....

KARMA3012: OMG WTF HAPPENED???

TRUMPETGRRL: IT WAS GOING FINE UNTIL HE BROKE UP WITH ME.

KARMA3012: OMFG?! AT PROM?

TRUMPETGRRL: YEP.

KARMA3012: DUDE.

KARMA3012: I AM SO SORRY. THAT IS JUST THE BIGGEST LOAD OF BULLSHIT...

TRUMPETGRRL: YEP.

KARMA3012: I AM SO SO SO SORRY, ELLIE... ARE YOU OKAY?

TRUMPETGRRL: I DON'T KNOW.

And I really didn't know. I could feel my fingers and my toes, but they didn't feel like they were parts of me. I felt my stomach roll over the gross banquet food, but it seemed distant, like something that was happening to someone else.

I knew my heart must be still beating, seeing as I was

alive and all, but I also knew for certain that it was broken into small bits that I wasn't sure could be reconstituted.

> KARMA3012: WELL ... TELL ME WHAT HE SAID.
> MAYBE THAT WILL HELP?
> TRUMPETGRRL: DOUBTFUL, BUT OK.

And I told her what had happened, as many of the exact words as I could remember. My fingers trembled a little over the sentence "I don't think I love you anymore," but I managed to type it out.

Strangely, seeing the words on the screen did kind of help. It put in stark relief exactly how awful and insensitive he had been, how he hadn't even treated me like a friend, let alone his *girlfriend* who he'd said he loved just a few short days ago. How this all came out of nowhere.

> TRUMPETGRRL: IT HAPPENED SO FAST ... ONE
> DAY HE LOVES ME AND THE NEXT DAY HE
> DOESN'T. HOW IS THAT POSSIBLE?
> KARMA3012: HMM ...
> KARMA3012: I'M NOT SURE IT IS POSSIBLE.
> TRUMPETGRRL: YOU THINK HE'S LYING? THAT
> HE DOES STILL LOVE ME?

My mangled heart shuddered a little bit when I imagined he was just breaking up with me because it was a misunderstanding, or that he was trying to protect me since I was leaving, or … something. Anything except what it actually appeared to be.

But Alex knew exactly what I was hoping.

> KARMA3012: SWEETIE, YOU CAN'T THINK THAT …
>
> KARMA3012: YOU CAN'T GIVE YOURSELF HOPE. WHAT YOU HAVE TO DO NOW IS GET OVER HIM.
>
> KARMA3012: HE WAS TOO YOUNG AND IMMATURE AND NOT RIGHT FOR YOU. HONESTLY, I DON'T THINK IT'S POSSIBLE FOR HIM TO STOP LOVING YOU BECAUSE I DON'T THINK HE ACTUALLY LOVED YOU.
>
> KARMA3012: AND IN FACT MAYBE YOU SHOULD BE GRATEFUL THAT HE TOOK CARE OF THIS FOR YOU. NOW IT'S OVER AND DONE WITH AND YOU CAN MOVE ON.

Well, she made it sound so damn easy.

> TRUMPETGRRL: MAYBE …
>
> TRUMPETGRRL: HOW??
>
> KARMA3012: BY GETTING OUT THERE AND MEETING NEW PEOPLE WHO ACTUALLY APPRECIATE YOU.
>
> TRUMPETGRRL: IT WAS ALMOST IMPOSSIBLE TO FIND ONE GUY WHO APPRECIATED ME … AND HE TURNED OUT TO BE LYING.

TrumpetGrrl: What makes you think I can find another?

Karma3012: Maybe you're not looking in the right places.

Karma3012: Or at the right kind of person.

TrumpetGrrl: ???

Karma3012: You're going to find lots of people who think you're amazing, Ellie.

Karma3012: You already found another one when you weren't even looking.

TrumpetGrrl: I have?

Karma3012: Yeah.

Karma3012: Me. Duh. Don't play dumb ... you know that I adore you.

I sat back in the chair, staring at the words on the screen. Alex, awesomer-than-awesome Alex, thought that I was amazing and she adored me! Just like how I thought SHE was amazing and adored HER!

I remembered how Alex hugged me when I left Covington, how it felt to be close to her. That it had been more comfortable and interesting and familiar than it had ever felt with Connor.

And it all clicked into place.

I *had* cheated on Connor. This was more than just a typical friendship. I was guilty.

All of a sudden, I was so tired that I could barely see straight.

TrumpetGrrl: I think I need to go to bed.

Karma3012: OK.

Karma3012: You'll get through this, I promise. Breakups suck donkey balls but I promise you'll survive.

Karma3012: And when you get to Covington, we'll have a drink and curse his name.

I laughed. Literally one hour after Connor had broken my heart, I actually laughed out loud.

I said good night and switched off my computer. Then I looked around my room, at all the small things that reminded me of Connor that I would have to get rid of—preferably in a blazing hot inferno in the fireplace.

But I couldn't deal with it then. I tore off my stupid purple dress, extracted the eight million bobby pins that were holding my hair together, and crawled into bed.

Sixteen

When I woke up the next morning, I didn't immediately remember what had happened. I blinked at the ceiling for a while, a sort of nagging emptiness behind my eyes making me think that something big had occurred. But what?

I sat straight up in bed with a yelp, clapping my hand over my mouth.

Connor broke up with me! Last night at prom! And also, Alex said that she adored me!

I looked wildly around the room, as if something might provide an answer or a remedy or maybe an escape hatch into some other dimension. Then there was a knock on the door.

"Ellie? Are you all right?" It was Mom. "Did you just yell something?"

"Um, sorry, bad dream," I called back to her. I wished it were just a dream.

"Can I come in? I want to hear about prom," she said. Without waiting for an answer, she opened the door.

She stood there, surveying the room—my pretty and expensive dress crumpled on the floor, bobby pins scattered on the dresser, strappy black shoes in the exact center of the carpet where someone would definitely trip over them.

Given that my room is usually so neat it resembles a museum, I think the mess tipped her off that something awful had happened.

And if it didn't, I'm sure my face revealed all.

"Ellie, what happened?" she asked softly.

I immediately crumpled into a ball of wet, slimy tears, hugging my legs to my chest.

"Oh, honey," she said, and came and sat on my bed. "That bad?"

I nodded, hiding my face in my hands.

"Do you want to talk about it?"

"I don't think so," I mumbled through my fingers.

"Are you … " she trailed off. "You're not hurt, right?"

Well, not in any outward way, though I still felt like pieces of my heart were floating freely in my body.

"No," I said. "Nothing like that."

"Okay," she said, softly stroking my back. "Whenever you do want to talk, let me know."

One thing I can say for my mom is that despite the fact she's nosy and sometimes kind of ridiculously uncool, she also knows when to leave me alone. She gave my back one last pat and left the room, softly closing the door behind her.

I briefly considered getting out of bed and facing the world, but soon decided it would be way too much work. I buried my face in my pillow and forced myself back to sleep.

I woke up blearily every twenty minutes or so, remembered what had happened, groaned, and passed out again. And I would have done that all day (and possibly for the rest of my life) if Kristen hadn't shown up.

She didn't even knock—she just stormed in the room. I opened my eyes and looked dully at her, not even bothering to sit up.

"What? The hell," she said.

"You heard."

"Yes I heard," she said. "And, honestly, I'd like to kill him. Would you mind if I killed him?"

I shrugged and closed my eyes again. "Not really."

"I mean, the damn nerve of that little boy! At prom! I just! Can't!" Kristen was sputtering uncontrollably.

"Eh," I said. "Whatever."

"*Whatever?*" Kristen said. "WHATEVER? What is *wrong* with you?"

Slowly I sat up, rubbing the sleep out of my eyes.

"I don't really want to talk about it," I said.

The expression on my face seemed to deflate Kristen a bit. "I'm sorry," she said. "Do you want me to leave?"

I shrugged again. "No, it's okay. Did you have a good time last night, at least?"

Kristen literally started glowing, as if someone had turned a hundred light bulbs on inside of her. She grinned, but then tried to cover it up when she looked at me.

"It was all right," she said casually.

I smiled wanly. "Oh, shut up."

"Okay, fine," she said. "Except for Connor-effing-Higgins, it was awesome."

"That's great," I said. "Really, that's great."

"I'm sorry?" she offered again.

"For what?" I asked. "Why should everyone else's night be ruined because he's an ass? I'm glad you had a good time."

Kristen looked relieved. "I guess I was sort of hoping you'd say that."

"So how'd it go with … um … " I trailed off. Last night was supposed to be the next big step forward in her relationship with Jake. I didn't particularly *want* to hear about it, but I knew that I had to at least ask.

"Oh, it didn't," she said with a sigh, sitting down in my desk chair. "But I'm glad."

"Really?"

"Yeah … timing seemed off or something."

"I hope it's not because of me," I said.

She looked on the verge of saying something, but then stopped.

"What?" I said.

"Well … maybe a little bit."

"Ugh," I said, putting my hand to my forehead. "I'm sorry. I knew how stoked you were about prom and everything and—"

"No, Ellie, stop," she interrupted. "It's just that I realized … as much as I love Jake, he could do the same thing as Connor did to you at, like, any moment. And I guess I just didn't feel ready anymore."

"Jake would never do what Connor did."

"But it's possible," Kristen said. "You would have never thought that Connor would have done that. And does anyone actually really know anyone else? Can we ever really be *sure* someone loves us?"

"Damn, Kris, look at you getting all philosophical," I said. "How did Jake feel about all this?"

"Oh, we didn't really talk about it." She grinned that glowy grin again. "We were too busy with … other stuff."

"Um, cool," I said, hoping she wouldn't really elaborate.

She shook her head. "But that's not important. What's important is you and how you're holding up."

"Actually, maybe not as bad as I'd have thought … "

It might have been a good time for me to bring up Alex, my confusion over my feelings for her, what that hug and kiss on the cheek back at Covington meant, the fact that we talked, like, every single day on Instant Messenger. I mean, Kristen was my best friend and I should have been able to just tell her about it.

But seeing her sitting at my desk, looking as cute and innocent as she always did, stopped me. What if it changed our friendship? What if she started freaking out that I might be attracted to her just because I was confused about my feelings for Alex?

And, God, what if she told people about it? Just the idea of that made me want to curl up into a ball and die.

"Really? What do you mean?" she asked. "I thought you and Connor were way in love. I thought you guys were going to get married or something."

I played with the corner of my comforter. It's true, I had thought about that. Marriage, I mean. As ridiculous as it sounded, it's hard not to imagine the long-term when you love someone as much as I thought I loved Connor.

And we had talked about it, too. Playfully, of course, but there was serious meaning behind it. And apparently that had all been a lie as well.

Suddenly I began to feel a lot worse. This Alex thing was silly and I was just trying to replace one thing with another. There was no hope. I was back at square one, all alone.

I don't think I love you anymore.

"No, it sucks a lot, actually," I said. "I think I might just be in shock."

Kristen seemed satisfied by this.

"Well, get out of bed."

"What?"

"You are not allowed to mope," she said. "And I know exactly what you need."

"To go back in time and never go out with him in the first place?" I suggested.

"No. Pancakes. You need pancakes," she declared. "And while we're eating them, we're going to discuss every single little last thing about that jerkoff that sucks. And then you will feel better."

She seemed so certain of this plan that I had no choice but to go along.

I obediently sat in Denny's and ate pancakes with her, listing off all the reasons why Connor sucked and how I'd be better off without him. But it was sort of like I was sleepwalking. I didn't actually internalize any of it. It didn't fill the gaping void in my brain where confidence in Connor's love for me used to live.

When I got home, Mom was waiting for me in the living room.

"Kristen told me a bit about what happened, that Connor broke up with you," Mom said as I slumped into a chair. "How are you doing?"

"Blah," I said. "And you can go ahead and say 'I told you so' if you want. I'm expecting it."

"Ellie, I'd never do that," she said.

"It seems like everyone else but me saw this coming," I said. "This is why almost everyone thought it was ridiculous for me to date a sophomore. Because they pull stupid stuff like this."

Mom was quiet for a moment and then said, "Well, you had to give it a shot, right?"

I looked up at her, surprised.

"I did?"

"Sure. Someone came along who saw something special in you, and you saw something special in him, and you had to give it a chance. There's nothing wrong with that. In fact, it's admirable."

"I ... guess?" I said.

"Change—stepping outside our comfort bubbles—is important, Ellie," she said. "Otherwise we never really figure out who we are."

"Wait a second," I said, narrowing my eyes. "Is this really about Covington?"

I couldn't believe she was taking advantage of my emotional ruin to give me another lecture about where I should go to college.

She sighed. "It's about life in general. What's the point if we don't take risks?"

"The point is we don't get hurt," I said. "If I hadn't risked it with Connor, I wouldn't be in so much pain right now. I wouldn't be so embarrassed and humiliated and feel so stupid. I don't know if it's worth it."

Mom shrugged. "It's hard to tell when you're right in the middle of it. But you don't know how it will even out in the end."

Again, I was suddenly very, very tired.

"Maybe," I said. "I think I need a nap."

We both stood up and she came over and gave me a tight hug.

"Let him go, Ellie," she said. "You're meant for bigger and better things."

Seventeen

The first week after Connor broke up with me sucked hardcore. It was a prolonged nightmare, like everything I hated about high school coming back tenfold to drive me even more insane than I already was.

People whispering, sometimes even laughing as I walked by them in the hallway.

Conversations going silent at the lunch table when I sat down.

That fakity-fake girly crap of "Ohmigod I'm SO sorry about what happened! How are you doing?" that came from every corner.

The extremely convoluted dance I had to do around the school during passing times to make sure I never ran into him.

And worst of all, the fact we still had to sit next to each other in symphonic band and jazz band.

How could I possibly move on, get over it, begin anew, when the person who had hurt me so terribly was around *all the time*? It was all I could do to get out of bed in the morning and put on clothes that approximately matched.

Kristen tried to help.

"Ellie, he's not worth your time worrying about," she repeated at least several times a day, ponytail bristling. She had taken Connor's actions as not just hurtful to me, but most definitely as a personal affront to her. "I'm *so* sorry that I set you guys up."

I nodded dully, chin cradled in my palms at the lunch table. Fortunately, Connor had quit sitting at the band table at lunch and found a dorky group of sophomore boys who didn't stare daggers at him like Kristen had taken to doing.

Though, frankly, it didn't really matter. I was still stuck sitting next to Connor for an hour a day in band. Even more on days when we had jazz band practice after school.

Connor tried to talk to me exactly once.

"Um…" he said eloquently, during a lull in jazz band rehearsal a few days after the breakup. "So…"

"Don't even," I said, not looking at him.

"Don't what?"

I glared at him briefly, wishing I could shoot fireballs from my corneas. "Don't even try and talk to me."

He sat there silent for a moment. Then, "So that's how it's going to be?"

"Yeah."

"We're not going to discuss this at all?"

"Connor," I spat, like his name was a swear word, "there is absolutely nothing to discuss. Unless you want to talk about what a child you are."

He looked down at his trumpet, compulsively pumped his third valve slide a few times, emptied his spit valve, and then looked at me with his gorgeous blue eyes.

For a brief moment, my heart jumped. What if he apologized? What if he said he'd been wrong? What if he said he *did* love me?

"Well, I guess there isn't anything to talk about then."

Kristen wouldn't give me any peace at lunch on Thursday.

"How dare he! How dare he act like he's all mature and that he actually cared about you and that he was capable of being a decent boyfriend," she said, her voice rising. "He's just a damn liar, is what he is."

She glared at Jake, who was sitting across the table.

"What did I do?" he asked, his mouth full of pretzels.

"Nothing," she said, ominously, "*yet*. But if you ever even think of trying to pull something like that on me, I'll…" She mimed grabbing a certain part of his male anatomy and twisting. "Which is what I think you should do to that jackhole, Ellie," she continued. "You should kick his ass. I can't believe you haven't already..."

She trailed off, her forehead wrinkled.

The point being that I hadn't been acting like myself since it happened. Which was true. I couldn't exactly muster up the will to be my old assertive self when it was all I could do to brush my teeth twice a day.

I shrugged. "Eh, whatever."

Kristen and Jake shared a worried glance.

"I don't know where you've gone, Ellie," she said. Jake nodded in agreement.

They just didn't get it. They didn't understand how it felt like my world had inverted and then imploded. All of the things I had taken to be true had turned out to be false. The sweet boyfriend who appeared to forgive me for all my faults, who loved me even though I could be difficult, who helped me see that I'd been closed off and remote and distrustful and had missed out on so much because of that.

Well, he turned out to be nothing but a big liar.

I felt like I was back to square one, back before I'd even met him. In fact, even suckier than that, because I knew what it was like to feel as if you were loved, that someone saw through your crap and still thought you were great—and then I'd lost it.

Or worse, just never actually had it to begin with.

Kristen put an arm around my shoulder. "Do you want us to beat him up for you? Because we totally will. It probably wouldn't even be that hard to do."

I attempted a wan smile, because I knew that's what she wanted, and shook my head.

"It's all right, guys," I said. "Seriously, I'm doing okay."

No one believed me and I didn't believe myself, but those were the right words to make it appear like I was moving on so everyone else could move on too. It's not like they could stay obsessed with my breakup for any length of time, anyway. Tons of other stuff was going on.

Sometimes even *I* forgot about the whole painful thing.

After all, I was still graduating in a little over a month. I still had to decide for certain which college I was going to. There was still the matter of the senior solo recital, the party my parents were planning to throw for me afterwards, three Advanced Placement tests to take, and wrapping up my high school life.

And then there was Alex, who had declared she was going to keep me sane from a distance. When I got home from school, in that lazy, late-afternoon time that I used to spend with Connor, I talked to her online.

TRUMPETGRRL: I KNOW THIS MIGHT SOUND KIND OF STUPID . . .

TRUMPETGRRL: BUT I THINK I SORT OF MISS YOU.

TRUMPETGRRL: IS THAT POSSIBLE?

KARMA3012: ☺ ☺ ☺

TRUMPETGRRL: IS THAT A YES?

It was hard for me to describe how I felt about Alex, even to myself in the quiet space of my own mind. I mean, obviously she was pretty much the coolest person ever. Not only would she say good, uplifting stuff like Kristen, about how I'd get through this and be stronger and that he didn't deserve me, but then we'd also talk about other things—books and music and what was going on in the world. My Winslow friends weren't dumb or anything, but they weren't all that interested in much besides the regular celebrity gossip, sports scores, and what was happening in the halls of the high school.

But Alex had a treasure trove, every single day, of awesome internet links to send me. About fascinating things that were happening in other countries, or beautiful pictures, or kick-ass websites.

Talking to her, I felt like the world was bigger and more full than it ever had felt before. That anything was possible.

And … yes. There was something more. I'd never felt this way about a friend before, certainly not a friend who was a girl. I kept imagining what she looked like, sitting at her computer. I paged through all her Facebook pictures, searching for clues about what she was doing … who she was doing it with.

One day I finally worked up the courage to ask her something that had been bothering me.

TrumpetGrrl: Are you dating anyone?

There was a long pause, and my cheeks burned as I waited for her to reply.

> KARMA3012: QUASI, I GUESS. THERE'S THIS GUY
> FROM THE COFFEE SHOP IN TOWN THAT I'M
> SORT OF HANGING OUT WITH. AND I'M SORT
> OF INTO THIS GIRL FROM MY ECON CLASS.
> BUT...

For some reason, my heart fell at the "quasi." And then I laughed, out loud, at myself. What was I expecting?

I just didn't like the idea of her being with anyone.

> KARMA3012: I SUPPOSE I'M NOT TOO INTO
> THAT.
> TRUMPETGRRL: WHAT?
> KARMA3012: OH, YOU KNOW. DATING.
> TRUMPETGRRL: WHY NOT?
> KARMA3012: IT'S COLLEGE, YOU KNOW?
> KARMA3012: IT'S NOT THE TIME TO BE TIED
> DOWN... IT'S THE TIME TO BE WILD. BE CRAZY.
> YOU'LL SEE WHEN YOU GET HERE.

"Can't wait," I said out loud.

> TRUMPETGRRL: WISH I COULD BE THERE RIGHT
> NOW.
> KARMA3012: I KNOW! BUT YOU WILL BE SOON
> ENOUGH. ONLY A FEW MONTHS TILL SEPTEMBER!

That felt like decades away...there was still so much to get through. Months and months of pre-college limbo.

And for some reason I couldn't figure out, I still hadn't sent in the acceptance forms to Covington. Or the housing packet to State. And it was definitely not because of Connor.

Or so I kept telling myself.

Eighteen

Almost two weeks after the World's Worst Prom Ever (courtesy of Connor Higgins—World's Worst Boyfriend), Mr. Barr called my name after symphonic band class.

"Can I see you for a moment?"

I involuntarily glanced over at Connor and caught him looking back at me. I raised my eyebrows, all *What the hell?*, and he shook his head slightly. Apparently Connor didn't know what was going on.

Or he could be lying. Wouldn't be the first time.

But if Mr. Barr was calling me into his office thinking we'd have a nice heart-to-heart about the state of my relationship with his nephew, he had another thing coming.

Oh, who was I kidding. Mr. Barr would probably be cool to talk to about it.

Mr. Barr hadn't said anything about our breakup, of course, though I had caught him giving the trumpet section quizzical looks in general. Especially since Connor and I had quit sharing a music stand and started ignoring each other.

As I put my trumpet away in the band locker room, I told Kristen and Jake I'd meet them in the cafeteria.

"What's going on?" asked Kristen, looking worried. "Is he going to, like, ask you about the—"

"Don't know," I said. "I sure hope not."

Mr. Barr closed his office door behind me. I sat down in the chair across from his desk, trying to mask my discomfort.

"Thanks for stopping in, Ellie," he said, steepling his fingers and smiling in his familiar, comforting way. I couldn't help but smile back. No matter what had transpired between Connor and me, Mr. Barr would always be my favorite teacher.

"Um, no problem," I said, crossing and then uncrossing my legs. "What's up?"

He tilted his head to the side. "How are you?"

This caught me off guard. "What?"

"Just a month or so left before graduation, right? How are you doing with that?"

"Oh … um … you know … " I said, shrugging.

"Not really," he replied. "It's been years and I think I've forgotten by now. Why don't you refresh my memory?"

I looked at Mr. Barr, with his warm brown eyes and quirky pointed mustache, the one teacher who had remained steady and routine during these entire four crazy years. And then I sighed.

"It's pretty much confusing, mostly."

He nodded. "In what way?"

I pushed ahead without thinking. Even if I blurted it all out now and totally embarrassed myself, it's not like I'd have to see him ever again after graduation.

"You know about me and Connor, right?" I said, quietly.

He gave me a morose sort of smile. "I gathered that things had ended."

"So... he didn't talk to you about it?" I hated myself for even asking the question. It shouldn't matter if he did, right? And of course Mr. Barr would never tell me, and he shouldn't, obviously. It was none of my business.

"Not really," he replied. "Well, he said that he wasn't hanging out with you anymore and that's the last word I heard on the subject."

"Oh," I said, feeling my shoulders slump a little. I mean, I was glad that Connor wasn't bad-mouthing me to his extended family, but at the same time, that was all he'd said about it?

"Was he... upset?" I asked quietly. "Because it's been kind of tough for me. Maybe you've noticed."

Mr. Barr nodded. "Yeah, he hasn't had a very easy time of it either."

I almost smiled with glee, but remembered that that wouldn't be an appropriate reaction.

"I'm sorry it didn't work out with you two," Mr. Barr continued. "But you're moving on to college, and I'm sure it was time."

"Right," I said, looking at my feet.

"Anyway, Ellie, I didn't call you in here to discuss your love life, believe it or not," he said. "I have a question."

"Yeah?"

"Have you decided what you're going to do next year?"

"Oh, *that*," I said. The topic that tied with Connor as the thing I least wanted to discuss. "No. No I haven't."

"As I remember when you had me write a letter of recommendation, you were planning on attending my fine alma mater and starting in the music education program, right?"

"Yeah, that was my plan at first," I said. "But then something else came up."

I told him about my surprise admission to Covington, the visit to the campus, how awesome it was and how at home I felt there. And now how I felt desperately confused as which way the correct path lay.

"I mean, I guess I've sort of always assumed I'd become a band director, since band is the only thing I've ever really been passionate about," I told him, and he smiled in a proud way. "That makes sense, right? How else do you decide what to do with your life except go for the thing that you know for a fact makes you happy? What else are you supposed to do?"

Mr. Barr shrugged. "That's a good way of looking at it, but it's not the only way."

"What do you mean?"

"Well, band makes you happy, but how do you know there aren't other things out there that could make you even happier?"

I made a noncommittal sound in the back of my throat.

"Why do you want to be a band director?" he asked. "What is it about band that satisfies you?"

I thought about it for a moment. "I like music, I guess, and charting out a show during marching band season and the football games. I like how everyone has to come together to become part of a larger whole. And . . . stuff."

I knew that this sounded lame.

"It sounds like you aren't completely sure," Mr. Barr pointed out.

"No, I am sure," I insisted. "It's just hard to completely describe it. But I know I'm definitely, definitely sure."

"Really?"

I sighed. "No, I'm not sure."

"That's what I thought."

"So I suppose you're going to tell me I shouldn't go to State, too," I said, a little bitterly. "And that I'd be a terrible band director."

Mr. Barr laughed. "No, nothing like that. I actually

wanted to offer you a chance to become more certain about that path. I'm heading out to a conference for a few days next week. It's bad timing because, as you well know, we have our final concert in a few weeks and we can't afford to waste that rehearsal time. I've requested a substitute teacher to try and keep things on track, but we both know how useful substitutes are for rehearsing."

"Heh," I said, remembering the last sub, who actually tried to get us to rehearse instead of just popping in a movie. I'm pretty sure she ended up screaming from the podium and possibly running from the room in tears. Jake had taken over.

"How would you feel about being in charge?"

I blinked at him. "Of the band?"

"Right. For the days that I'm gone."

"Um," was all I could think of to say in reply.

"I know it sounds intimidating, but it'd be a great experience for you, to find out more about what it's like to stand up there."

"But … I barely know how to conduct and I definitely can't read a score or … anything like that," I said. "How would that even work?"

"I know you don't know those things," he said. "And I don't expect you to. But standing up there on that podium with eighty people looking at you for direction isn't something you can imagine. You have to experience it. And if you're not sure if being a band director is for you, I think that would be an excellent way to try it out."

My heart was pounding. Maybe this had been the sign I was waiting for? The push in one direction or another?

"I'll give you the score to look at, and we can go over it before we leave," he continued. "I mean, you know the music so well, anyway. It would mostly just be a matter of keeping time. But don't feel like you have to take me up on this, if you're uncomfortable. It's really up to you."

"You honestly think I could do it?"

"I think you can do anything you set your mind to, Ellie," he said. "You're an incredibly determined person with a very bright future, no matter what path you take. But if you have questions about this particular direction, this might be a way to sort them out."

I nodded. "I guess you're right."

"Look, I won't be expecting you to perform miracles. But if you can run through each piece a few times and help keep the class under control, it would be a big help."

"Okay," I said slowly. I liked the idea of being a big help. "I'll do it."

"Excellent!" he said. "I was hoping you'd say yes."

I walked out of his office in a bit of a daze, wondering what I'd gotten myself into. Was I really going to pretend to be a band director? Was I really going to be able to put all my fears and insecurities about being up there in front of everyone aside, without any formal training?

"So what was that all about?" Kristen asked as I sat down at the lunch table.

I shrugged. "Not much. He asked me to fill in as the band director next week while he's gone at that conference."

"*What?*" said Kristen.

"Really?" Jake asked, from across the table.

"Yeah, don't make a big deal out of it," I said, glancing around to see if anyone else had overheard. "It's probably going to be a disaster."

"What do you mean? It's going to be awesome!" Kristen said. "You're going to get up there and realize you love it and then definitely come to State with us next year."

"Maybe," I said. "Or else I could realize what an idiot I am to even think I could ever be a band director and go become a hermit in the Upper Peninsula or something."

"Whatever, Ellie," said Jake. "Chill out. You're going to be great."

Sometimes Jake's simple confidence was refreshing. But other times, like today, it just seemed ignorant and uninformed. How the hell did he know it was going to be great?

"I'll see you guys later," I said, picking up my bag.

"Where are you going?" Kristen asked.

"I just need to be alone for a bit," I said, shrugging, and began to walk away.

"Hey, listen," Jake called after me. "If you want to go through some conducting stuff, I'd be glad to help."

I paused. That would be incredibly helpful. As a drum major, Jake knew about these things. I had learned a little bit about conducting and keeping time for running trumpet sectionals, but I had no idea what to do with my hands up in front of an entire band.

I turned around and smiled at him. "That'd be really great," I said. "Thanks."

"No prob," he said.

I was so lucky to have my friends. How could I even think about leaving them behind?

Nineteen

$\mathcal{I}$met up with Jake that Friday night to go over some conducting basics, and Saturday morning, the first thing I did was turn on my computer so I could tell Alex what had happened with band.

But as I sat there waiting for the computer to start up, I realized that she wasn't actually the person I wanted to talk to. I mean, she didn't even know anything about band.

The person who'd be most excited with me, I realized, was Connor.

I looked at my IM buddy list and fantasized briefly about adding his name back on so I could talk to him about it. He'd be so happy for me, right? Connor always said that I'd make a great band director and maybe seeing me go for my dreams would help him realize he loved me and...

Wait a second, just what the hell was I thinking? Get a grip, Ellie.

We could never go back to how things were. Not even if he did come to his senses. Right?

TrumpetGrrl: Guess what!!?!
Karma3012: What?

I told Alex about my conversation with Mr. Barr, how he was entrusting me to fill in while he was gone, and how I was pretty sure this was the key to me making a decision about where I should go next year.

There was a long pause, then—

Karma3012: Cool.

Her lack of enthusiasm was readily apparent in the absence of an exclamation point or further comment.

So I babbled on for a while longer, becoming more and more aware that I was basically talking to myself. She hardly responded to a thing I said.

TrumpetGrrl: Are you ok?
Karma3012: Eh.
TrumpetGrrl: What's up?
Karma3012: Well...
Karma3012: It didn't work out with that guy I was hanging out with.

Karma3012: And now it looks like you
won't be coming here next year.
Karma3012: and I guess I'm just sort of
bummed out in general.

An array of conflicting emotions swept over me. It didn't
work out with the guy she was seeing! Cool! More attention for me! She was bummed I might not go there next
year ... cool, and maybe kind of sad? Didn't she have all
her Covington friends?

And she was guilt-tripping me for maybe following
my dreams. Which actually made me feel kind of uncomfortable.

Couldn't just one single person in my life lay off and
let me figure this out without any guilt tripping? It always
turned into what my decision meant to them, not what it
meant to me.

TrumpetGrrl: Sorry you're bummed ...
TrumpetGrrl: And this doesn't mean I'm
definitely not coming to Covington.
TrumpetGrrl: Just that I'll be more cer-
tain of my decision if I do ...
Karma3012: I guess.

"ARGH!" I grunted out loud at the computer screen.
Maybe thinking that Alex could somehow magically fill
the void left by Connor was an incredibly stupid idea. If
boys were hard to figure out, I guess girls would be about

a million times more difficult. Seeing as we're the more advanced sex and all.

TRUMPETGRRL: I'M SORRY … I DIDN'T MEAN TO BE A DOWNER.

KARMA3012: IT'S OK … YOU DIDN'T MEAN IT.

KARMA3012: I THINK I JUST NEED TO GET AWAY FROM THIS TOWN FOR A WHILE.

KARMA3012: I LOVE IT HERE BUT SOMETIMES IT'S SERIOUSLY TOO SMALL.

KARMA3012: LIKE WHEN SOMETHING DOESN'T WORK OUT WITH SOMEONE ELSE WHO YOU STILL SEE AROUND ALL THE TIME. NOW I CAN'T EVEN GO TO MY FAVORITE COFFEE SHOP CUZ HE WORKED THERE.

TRUMPETGRRL: TELL ME ABOUT IT. THAT'S SOOO WHAT IT'S LIKE WITH CONNOR HERE. I DEFINITELY KNOW THE FEELING.

KARMA3012: HEH. STUPID SMALL-ISH TOWNS.

KARMA3012: I HAVE AN IDEA!

TRUMPETGRRL: WHAT?

KARMA3012: IT'S TOTALLY NOT SOMETHING YOU WOULD DO, SO I BET YOU'LL SAY NO.

TRUMPETGRRL: UM, TRY ME.

TRUMPETGRRL: RIGHT NOW I FEEL UP FOR JUST ABOUT ANYTHING.

TRUMPETGRRL: SERIOUSLY.

KARMA3012: OOOKAY. SO IT'S SATURDAY. AND WE SHOULD START DRIVING TOWARD

EACH OTHER, AND HANG OUT WHEREVER WE
MEET.

I stared at the screen, my mind instantly divided right
down the middle. Half of me couldn't imagine a sillier,
more ridiculous idea than just getting in the car and driving toward some unspecified point to meet some person
with whom I had some sort of unspecified relationship.

And the other half of me? Pretty much thought it was
the best idea ever.

> KARMA3012: SO???? YOU'RE TOTALLY FREAKING
> OUT OVER IT, AREN'T YOU.
> KARMA3012: I KNOW YOU ...

I began to hyperventilate, even though I hadn't done anything but sit still in a chair for twenty minutes.

It was one of those moments. I could feel that it was a
pivotal point in my own history. I knew I'd look back on
it forever, no matter which way I decided. This decision
mattered.

In the past, I hadn't often had the luxury of *knowing*
that a moment was pivotal ... they just sort of happened.
But this one I could fully appreciate in all its insanity.

> TRUMPETGRRL: WELL ...

I couldn't find the words to type after that. I looked at my
keyboard as if seeing it for the first time, like the answers
would magically illuminate themselves on the keys.

Karma3012: … …!

Karma3012: PLEASE Ellie it'd be so much fun!

And then, in a split second, I decided.

TrumpetGrrl: Sure, why not?

Karma3012: YAAYY!

Karma3012: Road trip!

And now that I'd decided, I couldn't imagine something that I wanted to do more than get in the car and leave right that second. I jumped up and looked around my room, wildly considering what I should bring. But then I remembered myself, and sat down at my computer.

TrumpetGrrl: Dude, what am I going to tell my parents??

TrumpetGrrl: I mean, they're fairly laid-back and all.

TrumpetGrrl: But I don't think they'd be so excited about this particular plan.

Or, really, lack of plan. Though to be honest, this was something my parents would be more likely to do than me. We'd taken all sorts of impromptu road trips as I was growing up, like when my dad decided he absolutely had to attend the Traverse City Cherry Festival or my mom required gelato from that one store in Chicago.

The unpredictability of which never failed to drive me kind of crazy.

On one memorable occasion, we started driving up north and were halfway to the Mackinac Bridge before my mom realized she had forgotten to wear or bring any shoes.

That sort of thing is what made me into the (slight) control freak that I am today. Somebody in the family had to be or else we'd end up wandering off the side of a cliff or something.

> KARMA3012: JUST TELL THEM THAT YOU'RE STAYING OVER AT YOUR FRIEND'S HOUSE.
> KARMA3012: THAT THERE'S A PARTY OR WHAT-EVER...
> KARMA3012: AND THEN TOMORROW TELL THEM YOU'RE GOING TO A MOVIE.
> KARMA3012: THEY'LL NEVER KNOW...I USED TO DO STUFF LIKE THAT ALL THE TIME.

Yeah, well, Alex was obviously a lot more gutsy and comfortable with spontaneity than me. I preferred an itinerary and maybe even a guidebook, and I was pretty sure I was going to be boring like that for the rest of my life.

For the rest of my life. Man, that sounded like a long time to be boring.

> TRUMPETGRRL: I DON'T KNOW...MAYBE I SHOULDN'T.

She replied instantly.

> KARMA3012: NOOO! YOU HAVE TO COME!

Karma3012: It'll be so much fun, I promise.

Karma3012: Don't you want to see me? And do something crazy and unexpected?

And I suppose that's what did it, what pushed me over the edge. Because I did want to see her. And I didn't want to be boring. I wanted her approval.

Karma3012: Just do it ☺

I decided the best course of action was to not think about it anymore. I was just going to tell my parents I was staying at Kristen's house, get in the car, and drive.

Karma3012: I just emailed you some Google map links so we can make sure we're on the same route.

Karma3012: But if we both drive about 70 mph, we'll probably meet somewhere around Faulkner, Ohio.

TrumpetGrrl: Man you work fast!

TrumpetGrrl: What are we going to do once we're there? What the hell is in Faulkner?

Karma3012: Does it matter?

TrumpetGrrl: I guess not ...

Karma3012: Well then, girl, GET IN THE CAR!!

And I did.

Twenty

My heart didn't stop pounding like a timpani drum until I was an hour outside of Winslow. I sort of fell into a lull then, listening to my U2 CD and not thinking about anything in particular.

"Sweetest Thing" came on. It had been the song Connor and I had called ours, back when he wasn't an asshole.

I skipped past it.

Kristen called my cell phone just as I was crossing the state line into Ohio.

"So what are you up to tonight?" she asked. "Because we need to get you out."

"Um, I'm out already," I said. "I'm driving."

"To where?"

"I'm not really sure."

"What's that supposed to mean?"

"I'm meeting a friend somewhere in Ohio."

"A friend? In Ohio?" she said. "Oh, God, Ellie. You didn't meet some strange old creepy dude on the Internet, did you? Haven't you seen those *Dateline* shows? Turn around right now!"

I laughed. "No, nothing like that. It's my friend Alex. The one I met when I visited Covington."

"Oh," she said, somehow managing to sound both relieved and pissed off. "I see."

"Yep."

There was silence on the line for a moment.

"Uh...just for fun or something?" she asked.

"I guess. We both sort of needed to get out of town."

"I see," she said again.

"You do?"

"Nope."

There was another uncomfortable silence.

"What do your parents think of this?" she asked.

"I sort of told them I was staying over at your house tonight."

"Really." It wasn't a question.

"Yeah...is that okay?" I had no idea why she was being so snappy.

"It's...whatever," she replied.

"Are you mad about something?" I asked. "Because it really seems like you are."

"No, I'm not mad," she said, sounding mad. "I just don't understand you."

"What do you mean?"

"This is totally not something you would do and plus, I've been hanging around, propping you up for weeks now, and you just head out to hang with her without telling anyone? You don't even know her. *I'm* your best friend."

This was sounding much like a conversation I'd have in fifth grade. And I was really glad not to be in fifth grade anymore.

"Dude, you're jealous?" I asked. "That's kind of silly."

"Is it? Really, I see," she said, speaking quickly. "You know what, Ellie? Sometimes I think I don't even know you. And sometimes I think that you should just go off to Covington with your new best friend and that would just be better for everyone."

"Kristen, what is your problem?" I said. "Why are you making this all about you?"

"I'm not. It's never about me. It's always about *you*, Ellie. It'd be a nice change if it *were* about me once in a while."

"I don't understand—"

She cut me off. "Talk to you later. If your parents call me, I'm not lying for you."

And she hung up on me.

"What the hell?" I said to the empty car, tossing my phone onto the passenger seat.

It was so infuriatingly childish. What, did Kristen think she had dibs on me or something? That I shouldn't be friends with other people too? That just because she had been pretty much my only girlfriend throughout high school that it had to stay that way forever?

"Whatever. I'm just not going to think about it," I said out loud.

Which I totally failed to do. I picked up the phone several times with the intention of calling Kristen and either making up or yelling at her, I wasn't sure which, so I put the phone back down every time.

Maybe it was for the best. Maybe we had to separate a bit. Maybe this was natural and normal.

But I still couldn't stop thinking about it.

The farthest I had ever driven by myself was an hour, and as the miles and hours drifted by, I sort of became hypnotized by the expressway. I put in a swing music CD to try and wake myself up a bit, but I drifted back into a reverie where the faces of Kristen and Connor and Alex all faded into one another.

What was I doing? Who were these people anyway?

Alex called me when I was about an hour away from our prearranged meeting point.

"I'm here!" she said.

I laughed. "You must have driven, like, ninety miles per hour or something."

"Yeah, pretty much," she said. "I was motivated."

By what? I wanted to ask, but didn't. I was nervous about seeing her, about how things would be between us.

Which was stupid, because we were friends, right? It's

not like I was driving to meet some guy who I wanted to hook up with. This was just Alex, the girl who had kept me sane for the past few weeks. And we were just doing something fun and spontaneous.

This didn't mean anything other than that. Right?

Alex gave me directions to the cheap motel where she had gotten a room.

"There's this awesome looking diner across the street," she said. "And the hotel has a bunch of movie channels. I think we should eat a pile of greasy food, get some ice cream, and watch some cheesy romantic comedies until 5 A.M. and forget about all our stupid boy problems. What do you think?"

"Sounds perfect," I said.

"Oh, I also brought a bottle of rum," she said. "So, yay!"

"Cool," I said, though the idea made me nervous. What if I got drunk and said something stupid? Or did something stupid? Or said and did something stupid at the same time?

I mean, of course that could happen any time, even without alcohol. But if my trip to Covington had taught me anything, it was the fact that when drinking was involved, things got a lot less predictable.

"So, see you soon, right?" she said.

"Yeah!" I replied, hoping I sounded confident.

We hung up and I eased my foot off the gas pedal, slowing down slightly. For some reason I didn't feel quite so eager to get to my destination.

I was mulling this over when my phone beeped. I had a text message.

No name came up but it was from a number that looked vaguely familiar. As soon as I saw the message, I knew why.

Can we talk? ASAP? Connor

He had assumed, correctly, that I had deleted his entry from my phone so his name wouldn't show up when I was scrolling through my contact list.

But, what the hell? He wanted to talk? And right *now*, when I was on my way to do ... whatever it was that I was on my way to do? Trying to be a different person who did crazy and unexpected things? Instead of contacting me at any other point in the past few weeks when I was still boring?

Seriously, universe?

I should have ignored him, of course. It's not like I owed him *anything*, let alone a reply. But I couldn't resist. I needed to know what he could possibly want to talk about.

And, let's be frank—especially if what he wanted to talk about was how much of an idiot he'd been.

So I one-handed texted him back, almost driving off the road in the process.

About what???

I managed to put the phone back down on the passenger seat. I tried to concentrate on driving but my eyes kept snapping back over to my phone.

Finally, after what felt like five or six hours, it beeped again.

Us.

That was the entirety of the text message … "us." As if there were such a thing, a unit consisting of a "me" plus "him" which equaled an "us."

Why in the world would he want to talk about *us* now, weeks after we broke up? I had moved on, right? I was off having adventures!

"Argh!" I said, and threw the phone back down on the seat. "I so do not need this."

I turned the music up louder and resolved not to think about anything until I got to Faulkner. And even then, I didn't really want to think. I just wanted to … be.

Which has always been nearly impossible for me, but no time like the present to practice.

I pulled up in front of the motel thirty minutes later, having successfully not texted Connor back. Faulkner wasn't much of a town … basically just a strip of fast-food joints and dollar stores lining a busy highway. It looked boring, but I wasn't there to be a tourist.

I turned the car off and sat there for a moment, staring dully at the motel's concrete wall, trying to figure out just what the hell I thought I was doing.

Doing *what*, though? It's not like this was a big deal that required lots of angst and mulling. I had left all that behind at home! I was just meeting a friend. And we were going to eat ice cream and watch movies and drink rum and forget about boys.

No big deal, Ellie, chill out.

So why couldn't I get out of the car?

Then there was a light tap on my window. I looked over, and Alex was leaning down and looking at me, beaming.

"Hey stranger!" she said, her voice slightly muted by the glass. "You getting out?"

Twenty-one

Alex was wearing dark blue jeans and a white tank top with light purple bra straps peeking out. She had made a paisley tie, like one my dad would wear on a day he went to court, into a headband, which held her hair back in two short, adorable pigtails.

It's nice to know some things can stay consistent. Such as the fact Alex would always look effortlessly cool in a way that made me feel totally inadequate.

But the way she was smiling let me know that that was stupid. It didn't matter that I was dressed in frayed jeans and a plain black T-shirt, both of which I'd probably owned since I was a freshman. She didn't care that I had a zit on my forehead and windblown tangles in my hair.

For some reason, she just looked really happy to see me.

I smiled back at her. "Of course I'm getting out!"

When I stepped out of the car, she squealed and wrapped me in a big hug, pinning my arms to my sides. "I can't believe you actually came! We're going to have so much fun!"

I laughed, feeling sort of fluttery as she took her arms away from me. "I can't really believe I came, either. I've never driven that far on my own before."

"There's a first time for everything," she declared. "Come on, I'm starving."

I grabbed my overnight bag and we walked to the room. "I hope it's cool that there's just a king-size bed," she said. "That was cheapest. I promise I don't kick."

"Um, sure," I said, because what else could I say? *I don't want to share a bed with you because I'm a freakin' weirdo?* "That's totally cool."

"Awesome," she said. "Well, it's not much, but it's not Covington or Winslow, so it'll do, right?"

The motel room was pretty hideous. There was a large stain underneath the air conditioner, and the teal and pink comforter on the bed had certainly seen better days. Like maybe in 1985.

I shuddered, my clean-freak brain wondering exactly what sorts of diseases were harbored in the fabric. But then I shook it off, and smiled at Alex. It really didn't matter.

Ten minutes later we were sitting in the greasy diner across the street from the motel. Faulkner was obviously not that big of a town, and when we walked in the room, everyone turned to stare at us.

Alex didn't even seem to notice. She probably was used to people looking at her, being beautiful and confident and all. She led us to a booth against the window and looked happily around her.

"Isn't this great? Small-town diners are so much fun," she said. Her grin was infectious.

A middle-aged woman in an incongruous pink dress and apron took our order as she snapped on her gum.

"Just keep the coffee coming," Alex said to her with a charming smile. "We have a long night ahead of us."

And even though the waitress looked tired and depressed and vaguely unhealthy, with huge bags under her eyes, she smiled back. Alex had that effect on people, I guess.

"So," she said when the waitress had left, "tell me how you're doing with this whole stupid boy situation. Have we figured out yet why boys are so stupid?"

"Not as far as I know," I said, shrugging. "Apparently they don't get better in college?"

"Eh," she said. "Some of them are, I guess. The vast majority haven't seemed to advance beyond high school. And the girls aren't that much better, to be honest."

I wanted to ask her more about that, about this strange and foreign concept of dating girls, but I couldn't. Not yet. So I changed the subject.

"Connor texted me on my way here," I told her.

"What?!" she burst out, so loudly that two old men with suspenders at the counter turned around and looked at us.

I told her about the messages, particularly his one-word reply, *us*.

"What the hell does that mean?" she said.

"I was hoping you'd know."

"Well, I know one thing," she said, angrily ripping her napkin into little bits. She was one of those people who couldn't just sit still. She would have been awful at standing at attention in marching band. "It means he's messing with your mind."

I hadn't thought about it that way. I'd assumed it was all benign.

"On purpose, you think?"

"Does it matter? If he succeeds in messing, it's irrelevant if the messing was intentional."

"Dude, that's deep," I told her. Sometimes I couldn't believe she was only a year older than me.

"And also true," she said. "If you ever feel like you're being manipulated, than you can just assume that you are. It doesn't matter if the other person intends the manipulation."

"I never thought about that," I said. "But you're totally right."

We sat in the diner for two hours, long after we finished our grilled cheese and pickle sandwiches and piles of French fries. Through four cups of coffee and two bathroom breaks.

"What happened with your guy?" I asked after we had suitably dissected Connor and his obnoxiousness.

"Oh, whatever," she said, shrugging, her purple bra strap sliding down and hanging off her shoulder. Whenever that happened to me, it looked stupid and sloppy, but on Alex it was cute. "He just wasn't someone I wanted to spend any more time on."

"Why not?"

"Because life is short," she said. "And he wasn't treating me the way I wanted to be treated. Also, he wasn't funny enough. I like people who can make me laugh."

I almost asked her if *I* made her laugh, but managed to hold back.

"Why did you like him in the first place?" I asked.

"He's smart and has a lot of interesting ideas," she said. "A poet, actually, which is always kind of sexy. And he had nice hands ... never underestimate the value of nice hands, and you can quote me on that."

I giggled.

"But then I realized he'd never actually left his hometown, you know? I mean, that's the only reason I met him—there isn't exactly a surplus of dudes in Covington. That's kind of a downside."

"True," I said, not adding that the absence of Y chromosomes was really kind of attractive at this post-Connor point in my life.

"And the ones you do meet are kind of hit or miss. I mean, this guy's parents work at the school and he grew up in town and just sort of stayed ... and he has all these great ideas and beautiful words. But what's the use of that if he never goes anywhere new, you know? I mean, how does he know who he actually is outside of Covington?"

She was looking at me with a bit of a knowing smile, and I caught on to what she was implying.

"What, you're thinking this applies to me?" I asked. "I'll end up like boring emo poetry guy if I stay near my hometown?"

"If the shoe fits," she said.

I threw a fry at her and she dodged it, laughing.

"If I go to State, yeah, I'll continue being a band geek, but in a new location with a changed set of circumstances," I pointed out. "That's entirely different."

"Not really," she said, "if you really look at it. It's you stagnating in the same identity. Just like him."

"Hmm," I replied noncommittally, trying not to be offended and studying the ketchup bottle. "What's so wrong with my identity?"

"Nothing at all," she said. "I think you're awesome. But don't you ever wonder if there's ... well, not necessarily *more*, but something *else* to you?"

"Maybe," I said, although the concept kind of bothered me.

It was cool—but also kind of strange—to be around Alex. She was just so ... smart. And, like, right *there*. Unlike Kristen and Jake, she didn't have all these preconceived notions of Who I Was coming from years and years of knowing me in all my annoying previous stages of life.

Like, if I said something to Kristen about how I'd started to like coffee, she'd roll her eyes and insinuate I was becoming pretentious because I used to only order hot chocolate. Once, when I showed up to school in my dad's old leather jacket because I thought it looked kind of cool, Jake made fun of me for going through an Elvis phase.

Instead of, you know, allowing for the possibility that drinking coffee and wearing a leather jacket *was* me. Like I never really had the option to change.

I'd never ordered coffee around Kristen again, and I'd hidden the jacket in my locker before second period.

I couldn't get away with anything around them ... around *anyone* who had known me since elementary school. I'd always get called out, and then I'd feel self-conscious and it just wasn't worth the trouble or embarrassment.

Easier to just stay the same.

Alex seemed to want to know me as exactly who I was, the Current and Changing Ellie. The one who wasn't entirely sure she wanted to be a band geek for the rest of her life but wasn't exactly sure who else she wanted to be, either.

And it's funny, but sitting there in that diner, it felt like she was the only person I could be real with. At least at that moment, as she looked at me like she knew me and believed I could be anyone I wanted.

"So what are you going to do about the dumb boy?"

she asked as she slurped down the last of her coffee. "Are you going to call him?"

I was anxiously tapping my fingers on the top of the table, jittery from the caffeine.

"What do you think I should do?"

She shrugged. "Hell if I know."

"What would you do if you were me?" I prodded.

"Ignore his worthless ass, have fun with Alex and forget about him," she said with a grin. "At least for a day."

I smiled back at her. "I guess I can try."

But without warning, an image popped into my head of Connor sitting alone in his room. Staring at his phone, waiting for my reply. Sad and lonely, hoping I would give him another chance.

And me chatting away here like he meant nothing to me.

But he was supposed to mean nothing now, right?

"Ellie, what are you thinking about?" Alex's voice snapped into my reverie. "Not about him, right?"

"Um..."

"Don't you dare even think about feeling guilty," she said, as if she could read my mind. "He treated you like crap and deserves nothing but the same from you."

"I guess..." I said doubtfully.

"Ugh, let's get out of here. We need to distract you."

Alex talked the waitress into giving us to-go containers of vanilla ice cream with little sides of hot fudge sauce. We ran back across the busy six-lane road to the motel, arms linked, Alex pausing to flip off the trucker who honked at us.

"Movies," she declared when we got back to the room. "Of the desperately cheesy variety."

"Yes," I said. "Most definitely."

We settled onto the bed, lying on our stomachs, spooning ice cream into our mouths. Alex ordered the most sappy love comedy on the pay-per-view menu, one of those ridiculous stories where some silly and contrived thing was keeping apart two people who were stupidly perfect for each other.

We'd glance over at each other at the corniest parts and giggle.

"I know what we're missing!" Alex said, somewhere around the point where the heroine began to realize she actually did totally love the hero even though he'd been a jerk to her. "Beverages!"

I paused the movie and she disappeared into the hall for a minute with the ice bucket, and came back with ice and a few cans of coke. And from her bag, she retrieved a bottle of rum.

"I totally stole it from Liz," she said, grinning. "But it's not my fault she leaves her dorm room open when she goes to class."

"Evil!" I said appreciatively.

Alex expertly mixed up two drinks and handed one to me. I almost took a gulp before she stopped me.

"Wait, we have to do a toast," she said.

"To what?" I asked, standing up.

Solemnly, she put her glass in the air. I followed. Little beads of condensation dripped off my cup and hit my bare toes.

"Here's to those who wish us well, and those who don't can go to hell," she said dramatically. We clinked glasses and both took a huge drink.

The rum burned from the tip of my tongue to the bottom of my stomach. I almost gagged, but managed to hold it in and smile at Alex.

"Lovely toast," I said. "Did you come up with that on the spot?"

"Nope, it's one of my dad's," she said. "His family is from Ireland, so he likes to pretend like he's still one with the motherland."

She said the last few words in an Irish brogue. It was adorable. Or maybe that was the rum talking already.

"Come on, let's see what happens next in the movie!" I said with fake enthusiasm. "I bet that they end up together in the end!"

We settled back down on the bed, drinks cradled carefully in front of us. After another half-hour and another rum and coke, my phone beeped with a text message.

I looked over at Alex, and she raised her eyebrows back at me.

"Well? You probably should look, don't you think?"

I set my drink on the bedside table and picked up my

phone. It was from Connor again. I took a deep breath and read the message.

PLEASE DON'T IGNORE ME. I REALLY NEED TO TALK TO YOU. IT'S IMPORTANT.

And then at the end he had typed in XOXO.

"What the hell," I said, and sighed.

"More head messing?" Alex asked.

I told her what the text message said, and she nodded sagely. "Ah, yes, the infamous guilt-trip tactic. He's a sly one, but we're on to him, right?"

I suddenly felt motivated to down the rest of my drink in one gulp. A little bit spilled out of the corners of my mouth, and I wiped my face with the back of my hand.

"I mean, seriously," I said, the words pouring out easier and easier. "What does he honestly think he's doing? Does he really think I'm going to want to talk to him after what he did? Does he think he can just beg and plead and act cute and I'll just forgive him? He's probably just horny or something."

"Probably," agreed Alex.

"I should write back, that's what I should do," I said, pacing around the room, pausing every few steps to take another sip. "I should write back and tell him exactly what kind of a jackass he is. Which is the big kind. The kind I don't tolerate."

Alex got off the bed, took my empty cup out of my hand, and went to mix me another drink.

"What else?" she said. "I think you're on a roll."

"I am!" I said. "I'm on a roll of not giving a shit anymore about what other people want and need out of me. I'm through with feeling weak and I'm through with putting up with everyone else's crap. Screw everyone else."

Even as I was saying this, I realized who I was acting like. And the person I was acting like was Ellie circa August of last year, right before I had met Connor. When I had been a self-professed bitch who never let anyone go beyond my obnoxious, mile-thick exterior into my vulnerable, gooey center.

I didn't like that hostile version of me. I had been glad to mostly get rid of her.

Well, back when there was someone around who said he was in love with me, I had been glad to be a little softer. But now, the vulnerable version of Ellie was kind of a liability. Such as when it became apparent Connor still had the ability to mess with my head.

"I think you've got it," Alex said, putting a fresh drink in my hand.

I shrugged, still pacing, feeling confused.

"Maybe."

"Ellie," she said, "stop thinking about it. Stop letting him ruin your night. Deal with it tomorrow. Don't be crazy."

I pivoted on one foot, almost falling in the process, and looked at her, ready to snap back *Easy for you to say, you're perfect and everyone likes you*. But then I saw that she probably didn't actually mean anything cruel by that.

She was just trying to help me. Right?

Just like Connor said he was trying to help you? A suspicious little voice said in the back of my head.

"Ugh, I don't know what to do," I said, putting my fingers up into my hair and pulling as if that would help me think better.

"Why do you have to do anything?" Alex asked. "Can't you just sit still?"

"What is it with you?" I snapped, and she winced. "Do you think you have all the answers or something?"

"No, of course I—"

"You're just like everyone else," I said, feeling only vaguely aware of the words that were coming out of my mouth. "You're just trying to make me into what you want. Which is ... I don't even know what that is. Why are you even hanging out with me? What is this?"

She looked hurt. "I thought we were friends."

"Yeah, friends," I said with a snort. "We hung out once before, and half that time you were being paid to give me a tour. We've just been talking online ever since. You think that makes this a real friendship?"

"Well, yeah," she said. She was biting her lip and I felt suddenly, sickly awful, like right after you realize you hit *reply all* on a group email when you didn't mean to. "Friends are people who care about each other. Who back each other up no matter how far away they are from each other. Don't you think that's us?"

I sat down on the far corner of the bed and put my head in my hands, not looking at her.

"Why do you even like me?" I said quietly. "It doesn't make any sense. *This* doesn't make any sense."

"What do you mean?" she said, crinkling her forehead. "You're awesome. We have stuff in common and we get along great. Of course it makes sense."

"But you're way too cool of a person to hang out with me," I said. This was approximately the moment I realized the rum was in full effect, as that is totally not something anyone should admit aloud. "I'm just some boring band geek from Michigan and you're..." I paused and looked over at her, and then quickly away again. "You're you."

"So what?" she said, sounding completely confused. "What's wrong with band geeks? And why shouldn't you be cool enough to hang out with me? We're both just people. That popularity shit is for high school."

"If you say so," I muttered.

Alex slid over on the bed and sat next to me, putting an arm around my shoulder. She was so close I could smell her coconut shampoo, but I still didn't look at her. Tears of the drunken kind were simmering behind my eyeballs. I didn't want to give them a chance to boil over.

"Ellie, you're an amazing person," she said, squeezing slightly with her arm. "I know that maybe you don't always see that, and I know that sometimes you're afraid to show people all your amazingness. But it's there. And once you get to Covington, you'll find more people who appreciate it. You know there's at least one person there already who thinks that."

I glanced over at her, at her solemn, kind face so close to mine, and just lost it completely. Sobbed, bawled, cried, wailed. The people in the next room must have thought there'd been a death in the family.

Alex rubbed my back in slow circles just like Connor used to do, and I lost it even more.

What the hell was I doing? Where did I think I was going? I couldn't see my future anymore … I felt completely out of control, careening through my life with no certainty or even a vague notion of where I'd end up in a few months.

When I'd calmed down a bit, Alex leaned over and rubbed her face on my arm, right where my T-shirt sleeve began. Her breath was warm on my skin but I shivered slightly, surprised.

"It's going to be okay," she said. "I promise."

I looked back at her, well aware that my face must have been snotty and blotchy and disgusting. She, as always, looked perfectly put together like a girl in a hipster magazine. But it didn't matter. She liked me.

My phone rang on the bedside table.

"Ignore it," Alex said. "And come here." She opened her arms and, after a pause, I leaned in to her embrace. And unlike the last time, at Covington, I didn't pull away.

Twenty-two

I woke up the next morning via sitting straight up in bed with sheer panic coursing through my veins.

Not the most pleasant way to greet the day, let me tell you.

For a minute, I had no idea where the hell I was. And more importantly, why the hell my head hurt so damn much.

And then, I remembered. Where I was, at least.

I blinked at the mini-blinds that were letting in slats of bright sunshine, then felt movement next to me in the bed. Alex was curled toward me, her hands clasped under her cheek, her light snoring barely audible over the hum of the air conditioner below the window.

God, what was I doing here? And what had happened?

I looked around the room and spotted the bottle of rum, three-quarters empty. Oh, that's just great, I thought. No wonder my head hurt so much.

Carefully, I lay back down, trying to move the bed as little as possible. I wasn't ready for Alex to wake up and look at me. Especially not before I'd pieced together what had happened.

There had been a movie, and then rum, and then Connor texting me again, and then Alex and I had... Christ, had we fought about something? And then I vaguely remembered tears.

I gingerly touched my face and felt the telltale, post-sob-fest burn, and tear crusts in the corners of my eyes.

How freaking embarrassing!

And then what happened? It was kind of a dark gray blur from there on out. Stupid rum!

Alex stirred again next to me, and suddenly the panic returned. I jumped out of bed, grabbed my overnight bag, and darted for the bathroom.

I managed to stay in there for twenty minutes, sitting on the edge of the bathtub with my forehead cradled in my hands until there was a knock on the door.

"Ellie, are you all right?" Alex asked, her voice muffled.

"No," I said, "I mean, yeah. Yeah, I'm fine."

"Are you sure?"

No.

"Yep," I replied.

"Are you really hungover? Because, dude, I sure am."

"Yeah, totally," I said.

There was a pause.

"Well, are you going to be too much longer? I have to pee."

"Oh, right, sure," I said, jumping up, irritated with myself. "I'm done now, actually."

I took a deep breath and opened the door. Alex was still wearing her white tank top, now with a pair of yoga pants.

She smiled at me. It was at least two hundred watts. "G'morning," she said, and then stepped around me. "I'll be out in a sec."

"Okay," I said.

I waited until she shut the door, and then tore around the room, changing my clothes and throwing everything in my bag. I opened my phone and froze up inside when I saw that my parents had called three times late last night and once this morning. I vaguely remember switching the ringer off at some point.

They wouldn't have called if they'd thought I was at Kristen's.

Oh, *shit*.

I was practically slobbering at the door, ready to run for the hills, when Alex came out of the bathroom. She looked at me holding my bag, bouncing from foot to foot.

"Are you ... leaving?"

"I have to get going," I said in a rush. "My parents called and I ... just need to go."

"Ellie, what's wrong?" she said. "Why are you freaking out?"

"Um..." I said, eloquently. "I'm...uh...I'm not freaking out."

"Right," she said, rolling her eyes. "Can't you just hold on for a second until I get ready?"

There was nothing in the world I wanted to do less, actually, but I nodded. "Okay."

I sat down on the edge of the bed and stared at the floor, tapping my foot, as Alex moved around me, packing up. She'd stop every so often and look in my direction, but I never looked back.

Finally, I glanced up at her and managed to spit out what was filling my head. "Alex? What happened last night?"

She stopped folding up her clothes and looked at me, her expression blank and unreadable.

"You don't remember?" she asked.

"Obviously not," I said.

"So I could probably tell you that anything happened? That you ended up streaking down the road and traumatizing the fine upstanding citizens of Faulkner, Ohio?" She had an amused glint in her eyes.

I did not find this funny. "I...guess you could tell me that. If you were a jerk."

She pursed her lips and nodded. "I see."

"So?" I said. "The truth?"

Alex stopped looking at me and began to stuff her clothes in her backpack. "You passed out."

For a moment I felt better. Then I realized something still could have happened before I passed out.

"But before I did that? I remember a movie, and then I think I was crying for some reason and then you were sitting next to me ... " I trailed off, my face feeling hot.

Alex stared at me. "Oh, I see," she said. "You wondering if anything happened ... between us?"

It was an instant relief to have her put words to my worries instead of having to say it myself. I just nodded.

And for the first time since I'd known her, Alex looked truly uncomfortable.

She didn't meet my eye as she said, "No, nothing happened."

"Seriously?"

"Yes," she said, now starting to sound a bit hostile. "Of course not."

"What do you mean, 'of course not'?" For some reason this was hurtful. Like in no universe could it ever occur that something more would go on between us.

"I mean, of course nothing happened between us because that would be stupid. We're just friends. You don't like girls. And I don't like you that way, anyway."

The feeling I got when she said that was remarkably similar to when Connor told me he didn't love me anymore. Some weird combination of a knife being twisted directly into the center of my ego while some option that I thought I'd had was being cut off forever.

She didn't like me like that. We were just friends.

Well, thank God I hadn't done anything to embarrass myself.

I put on a false smile. "That's good. Wouldn't want to go around ruining perfectly good friendships!" I forced myself to laugh, but it sounded more like a sickly hack.

"Right," she said.

"Okay, well," I stood up. "Guess I should get going. My parents called and I'm probably in for it."

"Ellie, wait." Her face looked pained. "I have to tell you something."

As soon as she said that, a rum-tinged memory from the night before rocketed into my head and exploded.

I had been lying on my side, near sleep, facing Alex. We had been very close, so close that I could feel her breath of my cheek. And she had tucked some of my hair behind my ear and had leaned forward and . . .

"You kissed me," I whispered.

She nodded, looking fearful. "I'm sorry. I was wasted too and . . . "

"You kissed me when I was drunk?"

"Ellie, look, it didn't mean anything, okay? It was just a . . . friendly kiss. You were crying and upset and then you sort of seemed like you wanted me to and . . . " she trailed off, searching my face.

"Is that all that happened?" I asked. "Just one kiss?"

"Yes, yes I swear. God, it's not like I took advantage of you or anything."

I paced up and down the room once, twice. My mind was uncharacteristically quiet and still. I couldn't figure out what I was thinking.

I turned back toward her. "But … we're still friends, right?"

Relief flooded Alex's face. "Of course we are! This won't change anything, I promise."

There was another brief pang of confusing disappointment.

But all I wanted was Alex as a friend, right? It's not like I was a lesbian, or even bisexual or anything. She was *just* a good friend. That's all I wanted her to be, and that's all she wanted me to be as well. Except … why would she have done that?

It was like with Connor, when things went further physically then I was really ready to deal with.

And the uncontrollable urge to get out of there and as far away as possible returned.

"Okay, good," I said with as much of a smile as I could muster. "All right, I really have to go. Five hours is a long drive."

She looked over my face again, studying it. "Thanks for coming."

I shifted to my other foot, uncomfortable. "Um, sure. It was … great to see you."

"And I just wanted to say," she said, and paused. "I just wanted to say that I think you're a really great person and I think you have an amazing future no matter where you go. But you just need to believe in yourself."

She was sounding totally like my mom did around the time I got my heart broken in ninth grade. When Mom was trying to convince me it wasn't the end of the world that I had been humiliated in front of the entire band.

That had been a really annoying time in my life.

"Thanks," I said, irritated. "But I do already. Believe in myself, I mean."

"Do you?" She stood up and started walking toward me. I edged in the direction of the door.

"Yes, I do. Do *you* believe in me?" I snapped. "Because apparently not."

"Of course I do," she said, stopping, her forehead wrinkling. "If you'd stop being so angry, that would help, too. And if you let other people help you instead of trying to push them away all the time you might be better off."

Now this was something I certainly didn't need.

"I appreciate your advice," I said. "But I don't need anyone's help."

She sighed and crossed her arms, looking resigned. "Fine, then, Ellie. Apparently you have all the answers. Goodbye."

It was a final kind of goodbye. A we'll-never-talk-again goodbye. And it felt exactly like someone kicking my ass out the door. I didn't want to listen to her stupid motivational speech, and it was like she suddenly hated me.

I looked at her for a moment, and she looked back.

And then she turned around and began packing her bag again. I watched her for a moment, part of me hoping she'd turn around and beg me not to go.

But she didn't. So I walked out of the room and quietly shut the door behind me.

Twenty-three

I waited until I was sufficiently calmed down to get out my phone and make the dreaded call to the parents.

"Hi Mom!" I said as cheerfully and innocently as possible. "What's up?"

"Elaine," she replied, and took a deep breath that was completely audible through the phone. "Just *where* the *hell* are you?"

It was the angriest I had ever heard her in my entire life. I almost laughed. Which would have been extremely ill-advised at that point.

"I ... um ... " I hesitated, hoping for hints about how much she knew.

"Connor called several times last night, saying he really needed to talk to you," Mom said snappily. "I said you were with Kristen, and he said that you weren't, that he'd talked to her and that she didn't know where you were."

Damn you, Kristen! Traitor!

"Oh," I said.

"So I called Kristen and she said the same thing to us. And then hung up. Quite rude, actually. Care to explain, then, exactly where you might be?"

I looked anxiously at a passing exit sign. "Um, Lewiston?"

"Lewiston, Michigan?"

"No … Ohio."

"Elaine! What are you doing in Ohio?"

I sighed. "Look, I'm sorry for lying to you, Mom … I was just visiting a friend. My friend Alex."

"A BOY?" she burst out. "Because Kristen said something about a man from the Internet and I—"

I laughed. "God, no. I was visiting Alex … remember her? The girl from Covington?"

"Alex?" Mom seemed both confused and relieved at the same time. "The nice girl with the short dark hair? Who wanted to be a lawyer?"

I took the phone away from my ear and stared at it for a moment, wondering if this was a practical joke.

"Uh, yeah, I guess," I said, putting the phone back.

"Why did you need to meet her? And why didn't you tell us?" Mom seemed oddly less angry now that she knew I had been with Alex. "We probably would have been fine with it if we'd known where you were."

I decided to just be honest. "I wanted to do something...crazy. You know? I wanted to be spontaneous and take a risk and be a little wild. I've never been wild. You know that, Mom."

I could almost hear her nodding. This was her language. "Ellie, I always felt you were an old soul who didn't get enough of a chance to let loose."

"See? You know what I'm talking about."

"But that doesn't mean," she said, anger creeping back into her voice, "that you are *allowed* to be *unsafe!* We had no idea where you were! What if you had gotten in an accident? Or needed us for something? Or...I don't know! You've just never done anything like this before and we don't even know what to think!"

Mom sounded close to tears. I was kind of shocked, frankly. She'd never been one to cry over me. More often she snapped at me or guilt-tripped me or glossed over things. None of this crying stuff.

"Mom, I'm sorry," I said, feeling completely awful. "I didn't realize—"

"Are you going to act like this when you go to college?" She was definitely crying now. "Didn't I teach you anything about being responsible? Have I been a terrible mother?"

What. The. Hell.

"No, Mom!" I said. "You've been great! I just...I don't know what I was thinking. I *wasn't* thinking. I promise that I'll be safe when I go to college. And I should have told you. I'm really, really sorry."

Which was not a lie. If I had just told her where I was going instead of trying to be sly, we wouldn't be having this extremely awkward conversation right now.

She sniffled into the phone. "Really?"

I felt like I was acting like HER parent. "Yes, I promise. You've been a wonderful mother."

There was a silence, punctuated by the obvious sound of her wiping her nose with a tissue. "Thank you."

"You're welcome," I said, cringing at myself.

We both paused. For a second I wondered if she had hung up on me completely.

"How long will it be until you get home?" she finally asked.

"Um . . . three hours?"

"Elaine! How far away were you?"

"In Faulkner. Halfway between Winslow and Covington."

"Oh, I see," she said. "Just to meet Alex?"

"Yeah," I said, and sighed involuntarily.

"What, didn't it go well?" she asked.

Oh, Christ, could anything be more embarrassing?

But I needed to talk to *someone* about it. Kristen was obviously not going to be a willing ear, and it's not like I could talk to Jake—who would probably go all wide-eyed and demand to know what base we had gotten to and if maybe next time we could take pictures.

But if there was one thing I knew about my mom, it was that she was liberal to a damn fault. In fact, it would probably make her *happy* if I turned out to be gay. Then she could brag to all her liberal-to-a-fault friends and they would ooh and ahh over how freakin' accepting she was of the situation.

Still, though, it was nice to know I wouldn't be disowned.

"It went okay, I guess," I said.

"Just okay?"

"Well … I don't know. I'm not sure what I was expecting and it turned out to be weird and I don't know exactly what we are and … I don't know."

"What you are?" she said, and then took a deep breath. "Is there something more between you and Alex than just friendship? Because I have to say, Dad and I got a … vibe."

"You got a *vibe?*" I said in disbelief.

"Yes. That perhaps she had taken more than just a friendly interest in you. And maybe you in her, as well."

Why did I have to be cursed with a mother who was occasionally so perceptive?

"Maybe … " I said, trailing off uncomfortably.

She was silent, waiting for me to elaborate.

"I don't know," I said. "I mean, I really like her and it was kind of confusing."

"Mmm-hmm," Mom said, egging me on.

"But now I don't know. I think she's awesome but I don't know in what way I think she's awesome and she makes me feel kind of weird and I feel pretty stupid and I kind of hate myself over the whole thing." I let the words tumble out like an avalanche. "Even though I sort of think I really like her."

Saying it out loud was like making it real. Pinocchio made into a real boy. My feelings for Alex put into words. To my mother!

"Oh, Ellie," Mom said. "You know what love is all about, right? You've been there before."

It was kind of the first time she'd acknowledged that what happened between me and Connor was something that could be called "love."

"I guess."

"It's about realizing what kind of person you want and acting like a fool and screwing up and everyone else screwing up too and eventually, in the end, you find the person who accepts all your screw-ups and whose screw-ups don't drive you insane and who you can't live without and that … *that* is love. It's definitely not about hating yourself."

Which was, perhaps, one of the most sane and reasonable thing I had ever heard my mom say.

"Really?" I asked in a small voice.

"That's been my experience, anyway," she said. "And I know I'm old and boring and maybe a little bit crazy, but I've got quite a bit of experience. And this is something I know. Love is both the easiest thing in the world and the most difficult."

"You got that right," I muttered.

"You're a smart girl, Ellie," she said. "You'll figure it out."

I wasn't so sure about that, but her confidence was nice, I guess.

"Thanks, Mom."

"Hurry home."

"I will."

Twenty-four

I wasn't sure what to do with myself once I got home. Well, first I had to face my parents, who were waiting for me in the living room. They sat close to each other on the couch, looking weirdly stiff.

They also looked uncomfortable and unsure of themselves, which isn't much of a surprise considering this was probably the only time I'd gotten in real trouble my whole life. I mean, I'd gotten in trouble a lot for running my mouth, but not ever for actually *doing* something wrong.

"I'm sorry, guys," I said before they even had the chance to yell. "I know it was a stupid thing to do, leaving town without telling anyone where I was going, and I won't do it again."

They looked instantly deflated.

"Well, damn straight you won't do it again," said Dad, trying to look stern, which I knew for a fact was totally all for show. Because all three of us knew that I'd be moving away from home in a few short months, and they'd have no day-to-day control over me then.

"Elaine..." said Mom, trailing off. I looked at her.

"Yeah?"

"Do you want to talk about it? About where you were?"

Dad glanced over at her in surprise. Apparently this hadn't been a previously agreed-upon talking point.

And I knew she was referring to what we'd discussed in the car.

Which, obviously, I now completely regretted bringing up.

"No, not really," I said. Not only did I not want to discuss it with my parents, I didn't really want to think about it within my own brain. I'd managed to barely consider it during the entire rest of the drive, except for one ill-considered text message to Alex when I reached the Winslow city limits, tersely informing her that I'd made it home safely.

She hadn't replied.

"Okay," Mom said. "If you're sure."

The three of us looked at each other for a few moments.

"Um, anything else?" I asked. "Are you going to punish me or something?"

They glanced at each other. "Well," said Dad, "we didn't think there would be much of a point. We just wanted you to know..."

"That we're disappointed in how you acted," Mom finished decisively. "We expected more of you."

Honestly, I would have preferred to be grounded or have my cell phone taken away or be locked in a cupboard with some rabid spider monkeys for an hour or something. Parental guilt trips are the absolute worst.

"Okay," I said. "I'm sorry I let you down..."

There was another uncomfortable silence.

"So, anyway," I said, "guess I'll just... go to my room?"

They both shrugged.

"Okay," I said. I started to walk out of the room, then paused. "I'm sorry, guys."

They didn't reply, just looked steadily back at me. I left, cringing as I ran up the stairs.

Back in my room, though, I had no idea what to do with myself. I got out my trumpet and half-heartedly worked my way through my senior solo piece. It was desperately mediocre. I didn't have all the rhythms down and I knew that I needed to get to work with my accompanist, but I just felt so unmotivated.

Which wasn't exactly going to work if I was still planning on getting that scholarship to State. Which was beginning to look a little more attractive now that things were weird and stupid with Alex.

Eventually, tired out, I put my trumpet away and sat down on the bed. I wanted to talk to someone. But apparently I had pissed off and/or disappointed just about everyone in my life. Except for...

I turned on my computer.

TrumpetGrrl: Hey Jake! What up?

There was a long pause, during which I wondered if I had done something to piss *him* off as well. But then ...

MajorJake: Dude.
TrumpetGrrl: What?
MajorJake: WTF. What kind of trouble have you gotten urself into?
TrumpetGrrl: Um ... how much have you heard?
MajorJake: Well, PLENTY from Kris, lemme tell ya.
TrumpetGrrl: Yeah ... she sort of hates me now, huh?
MajorJake: Hate is such a strong word.
TrumpetGrrl: Maybe not in this case.
MajorJake: Maybe not.

I paused and bit my lip. My friendship with Jake had been a little strange since he and Kristen started dating. Well, not strange so much as different, in subtle and confusing ways. We couldn't do the same amount of flirty teasing, or really hang out just the two of us, because it just felt ... weird.

Not that I'd ever thought of Jake as anything except a pseudo-brother, but things had changed, no doubt about it. And I never knew exactly how to act. As if he was an extension of Kristen, or entirely his own person? I had to assume that they shared everything... telling one of them something was just like telling both of them.

> TrumpetGrrl: So is she going to forgive me?

I had already decided it wasn't worth staying all huffy about her not lying to the parents for me. After all, it's not like I really got into trouble. And I felt guilty for not telling her about it either.

I felt guilty about a lot of stuff, actually. Why had I listened to Alex and left town without telling anyone?

> MajorJake: Probably. I think she's cooled off. You should call her.
> MajorJake: You know it's just because she's gonna miss you, right?
> MajorJake: We both will... I mean, if you end up not going to State.
> TrumpetGrrl: Yeah.
> TrumpetGrrl: I just wish she weren't so... I don't know.
> MajorJake: Yeah, know what you mean.
> MajorJake: But... both of you can be kinda... opinionated.
> MajorJake: But that's what makes you such good friends.

MajorJake: I hope we stay buds no matter
   what.
TrumpetGrrl: Dude, of course we will!

Feeling marginally better about the Kristen situation, at least, I gave her a call to convince her to go out to coffee.

"I'm surprised you're even talking to me," she said, sounding slightly guilty herself. "I mean, aren't you mad I sort of . . . ratted you out?"

"Eh," I said. "It wasn't really ratting out. You just said you didn't know where I was. And I should have told you, anyway."

"Yeah, you should have."

"Sorry, Kris." I thought about what Alex had accused me of, that I didn't let people help me or know me and never let down my defenses. "You know I think you're a great friend, right? And that I don't know how I would have made it through the past few weeks without you? You've been awesome and I'm lucky to have you."

There was a kind of surprised silence on the other end of the line.

"Really?" she finally said.

"Yeah, totally," I replied.

"Um . . . thanks," she said. "Wow."

We went out for coffee and it was like nothing had ever happened.

I told her about how Connor had contacted me and she was in complete agreement with Alex.

"Forget him," she said decisively. "He doesn't deserve a second chance."

"If that's even what he wanted," I said sullenly, sipping my coffee (which, I guess I should point out, Kristen did not make fun of when I ordered; maybe I did just read too much into what people said). "But what if—"

"Ellie, there are no 'but what ifs' in this case. There isn't anything he can say that should change anything."

"I guess."

I still wasn't convinced. He obviously still had some sort of power over me, even if he'd treated me terribly.

I found it funny and sad how that worked...that because I'd loved him once, I couldn't block him completely out of my heart. But I don't think normal people can just turn off their emotions like a faucet. Obviously, I would still have some residual feelings for him. A part of me said that I always would, even when I was eighty years old.

"Anyway," I said, by way of changing the subject.

"Anyway," she repeated. "So you visited your friend Alex, huh?"

This was very fragile ice to be walking upon. I could almost feel it cracking under my feet.

"Yeah."

"How'd that go?" she asked, far too casually.

I took a deep breath and then said, "Kind of weird."

Kristen looked over at me curiously. "What do you mean?"

"Well, I don't know..." I filled her in on some of what

had happened. I definitely left out the part where Alex had drunkenly kissed me, but I told Kristen how we had sort of fought, how Alex thought I should go to Covington and it just felt like more pressure and kind of like a manipulation.

"You know, that sort of manipulation sounds like something Nathan would have pulled last fall," Kristen said. "And pressuring you like that was pretty crappy of her."

I gave her a level look.

"And I'm pressuring you too, aren't I?" she asked.

"Um, yeah ... sort of. But it's okay," I replied. "I mean I can't blame you, or Alex, or my parents, or Mr. Barr or anyone for trying to help, I guess. That's all anyone is trying to do. Help, I mean."

"That's true."

"But I just don't know what to do, yet, you know? I feel like I'm waiting for a sign."

"Like what?" She looked at me skeptically. "A booming voice out of the sky? A prophetic dream?"

"Heh, no," I said. "Although one of those would make it easier. I guess ... I'll know it when I see it. Or feel it or experience it. Or whatever."

"Hmm ... Good luck with that."

"Yeah, thanks. I need it."

That night, I finally texted Connor back.

I NEED SOME TIME. WILL LET YOU KNOW WHEN
I'M READY TO TALK.

Twenty-five

The morning before my first attempt at pretending like I was a band director, I couldn't even eat breakfast. It was a worse anxiety than what came before a chair audition, or the first day of a new school year, or a giant AP Calc test.

This time, it seemed to really, really matter.

I got out of my third-hour class early in order to be in the band room a few minutes ahead of everyone else. The substitute teacher was sitting in the chair of the first flute, ringing her hands. She looked very young, barely older than me.

"Oh, are you Ellie?" she said, and I nodded. "Thank goodness, I was so scared you wouldn't show up and I'd have to figure out what to do with this class!"

I smiled at her. "Nope, here I am."

"It's my first week subbing," she told me. "I have no idea what I'm doing."

"Well, that makes two of us!" I said cheerfully. It made me feel better to see someone who was more nervous than I was.

"So you'll be directing or whatever?" she asked. "And they'll be playing?"

"Yeah, that's what bands generally do." I held back a laugh. "Maybe you should sit over there." I indicated a row of extra chairs by the back blackboard.

"Okay," she said meekly, and held up a class roster. "But I have to take attend—"

"I can do that," I said, taking it from her before she could object. "I know everyone. It'll be easier that way."

"All right." She looked a little relieved. "Thank you."

Band kids started filtering in and heading toward the instrument storage room, some of them casting me amused glances. Mr. Barr had told everyone that I'd be filling in as director, but the reality didn't sink in, probably, until they saw me standing on the podium.

I watched everyone get their stuff and tried to study the score a little more. I had pored over it for the past few days, trying to understand at least a little bit about how the instruments fit together on paper instead of just by ear. Jake had tutored me a bit more on how to keep passable time with a conductor's baton.

I mean, I was as prepared as possible.

But my knees were shaking anyway.

Kristen and Jake were in their seats promptly, looking at me with suppressed smiles. Some other kids were slower moving, though, and eventually I tapped my baton on the edge of the music stand.

"Can we all get seated?" I yelled.

Sixty pairs of eyes were instantly on me. It felt like they were burning little holes directly onto my skin. I cringed.

"Please?" I added, and cringed again.

I mentally cursed myself for showing weakness already. Especially after I heard a chorus of giggles.

Okay, okay. I could totally do this. Being a band director was what I might want to do for the rest of my life—I had to give it a shot.

"All right, we'll be starting with 'English Suite,'" I said, as if they hadn't laughed and were all paying rapt attention to me. "But let's warm up first."

Nothing. I might as well have been talking to myself. The drummers were talking loudly in the back, one of them idly tapping away on a snare. The tubas sounded like they were holding a competition as to who could make a sound most like a fart. The trombones hadn't even bothered getting their instruments out yet.

The only sections that were paying attention were the trumpets and the alto saxes, and that's just because Jake and Kristen were in the process of issuing violent threats to anyone nearby who wasn't sitting quietly.

I glanced at Connor, sitting next to my empty chair

in the trumpet section, but he was not looking back. He seemed kind of uncomfortable, his shoulders hunched over in the way I knew they did when he was anxious, but he was not offering any support, even in the form of a helpful smile.

He probably thought I was a joke.

An instant desire to burst into dramatic tears almost won out, but I managed to push it down. No! I wasn't going to let these... these *kids* win! I was in charge here! This was my show!

I took a deep breath, got out my biggest and bitchi-est section leader voice, and boomed, "Take your seats for warm-ups or I will mark you tardy." I paused for dramatic effect. "And make you run *laps!*"

The substitute teacher coughed uncomfortably from the back of the room.

Technically, I wasn't sure I could follow through with that threat. It wasn't marching season anymore, and there was no reason for us to go outside. But by God I was going to use whatever means necessary to get control of the situation.

And it just so happened to get through to them. After all, the trumpets knew, firsthand, that I was always more than happy to make good on my laps threat, and the rest of the band had seen that as well. They sat down, a few more slowly than others, and soon everyone was looking at me.

Suddenly I was even more nervous than I had been when no one was paying attention.

"Okay," I said. "That's better. Let's warm up with a B-flat scale."

I raised my hands, the sign for the band to lift their instruments and play, and then slowly conducted a scale. There were a few intentionally out-of-tune and blaring notes, particularly from the Brandi Jenkins area of the room, but overall…

Overall…

It was *awesome*. To be in front of all those instruments blending together, those eyes on me, watching my hands, responding to how I moved, doing what I wanted them to do.

I realized, halfway through the scale, that I had a stupid grin on my face and tried to subdue it, but a few seconds later it was back—so I quit trying. I glanced at Connor again, and he was staring at me intently.

And could I be I mistaken, or was his mouth also curved into a smile around his mouthpiece?

We ran through another scale and then I nodded toward Ben, the first-chair clarinet player. He stood up and played a note for the band to tune their instruments to while I quickly ran through the attendance list.

Since I knew every single person there by their full names, as well as what their parents looked like, how good they were at their respective instruments, and practically what their favorite colors were, this wasn't hard to do.

That's what happens when you're involved in the same activity for seven years straight (counting middle school).

I spread out the score to "English Suite," one of the pieces we were playing for our final concert, in front of me. Then I looked up at the band. They looked back at me.

"Let's start at the beginning," I suggested, and raised my arms again.

I walked toward the cafeteria an hour later, every molecule in my body buzzing. It was like the first time I made out with Connor, except better because I could see myself doing this in public all day, every day, forever.

It hadn't been perfect. Some smartass from the trombone section had thrown a gum wrapper at me when I was working through a segment with the clarinets. I had to yell at the drummers once for talking too loudly, and I wasn't certain I had actually accomplished anything productive. It had been more like marking time.

But that was okay, because it had also been awesome... the feeling of being in control of the band; of having their eyes on me; of creating music, the waves of sound rolling through me as I stood on the podium. The experience had been unlike anything I'd ever felt in my life.

Better than most things, in fact.

Possibly even better than walking the hallowed halls of Covington.

"Dude," said Jake as I sat down at the table. "Good job."

I couldn't help grinning like a fool. "Really? You think so?"

"Totally," Kristen chimed in. I looked down the row of people at the table, and they were all looking at me with expressions of admiration. Some were more grudging than others, but in general, everyone seemed positive.

"I mean, not as good as Mr. Barr or anything," said Aaron, shrugging his shoulders. Kristen hit him on the arm. "Ow! But good for someone who didn't know what they were doing! Okay? Jeez."

"Thanks," I said, feeling giddy.

"So," Jake said, looking at me with raised eyebrows. "Did that make anything more clear?"

I stalled for time by taking a big bite of my sandwich.

"Mmmhmm," I mumbled through it.

"What? It did?" Kristen burst out.

I shrugged. "Yeah, I guess it did."

"And?" she said, her eyes wide.

"I'm going to try for the scholarship at the solo recital," I said. "I'm at least going to give it a shot."

"Yay!" Kristen yelled happily, so loud that most of the surrounding tables turned and looked at us. "That's the best news ever!"

I laughed uncomfortably.

Because that senior solo recital—the one at which I was supposed to perform a fabulous trumpet solo that would earn me a scholarship and take me to State to become a band director? Well, with one thing or another—things named Covington and Alex and Connor—I had hardly practiced at all.

And the recital was this weekend.

Twenty-six

$\mathcal{Q}$ went home and paced around my room, trying to figure out what I was going to do. There wasn't anything in the world I hated more than being unprepared. I'd had nightmares about it … of showing up in class and not having studied for a test, of meeting someone who knew all about me and I didn't know anything about them …

Of being in solo recitals but not having practiced.

I needed help—that was for sure. Someone who could kick my ass into action with the solo. I cursed myself for not finding a new teacher when my former private trumpet teacher had moved away last year. Because there was only one other person I could think of who could help me.

I unblocked Connor's name on my Instant Messenger buddy list.

He didn't come online for a long time, and I made up all sorts of elaborate explanations that involved some cute sophomore girl who he'd fallen in love with in a matter of weeks and would probably end up marrying.

Or, less dramatically, maybe he had given up online activity altogether after I blocked him, and this was pointless. Maybe I should text him, or swallow my pride and call him...

Just then, his name popped up on my buddy list.

I watched it for a few minutes, willing it to start flickering to indicate he was writing to me. I mean, wouldn't he be surprised that after all these weeks my name would show up on his buddy list again? Wouldn't he message me right away?

Nothing. Maybe he'd taken me off his list too.

I sighed, stood up, and went downstairs to grab a snack. If he hadn't written to me by the time I got back, I promised myself I would sign off. I'd grow some balls and approach him at school if need be. I would *not* sit there and stare at a computer screen all night waiting for him to notice me!

He had not messaged me by the time I got back.

I sat in my desk chair, biting down my thumbnail for a good five minutes, and then doubled clicked on his name to bring up a new chat window.

TRUMPETGRRL: HEY.

When no reply came within the first ten seconds, I pan-
icked and had to get up and pace around my room for a
few minutes. What the hell! Why had I done that! HE had
broken up with ME! What was I thinking messaging him?
This totally made me pathetic and desperate and—

When I sat back down, the Instant Messenger window
was blinking. He had replied.

C-Note: Wow. Hey. What's up?

"Yes!" I said out loud, throwing my arms up in the air like
a football referee signaling a touchdown.

But, holy crap, what was I going to say now that I had
his attention??

I decided to play it casual.

TrumpetGrrl: Eh. You know. Usual.

I stared at the screen as if it were a mystical oracle until he
wrote back.

C-Note: Um, I guess.
C-Note: So…

He didn't say anything else. Just left it at that. For three
whole minutes.

"So what?!" I said to my empty room. "Don't leave me
hanging, you jerk!"

Of course, I gave in eventually.

TrumpetGrrl: So what?

C-Note: So you're ready to talk to me now?
Or do you need something.

Shit, the boy knew me way too well. He definitely knew
something was up.

TrumpetGrrl: Just wanted to see how it
was going.

TrumpetGrrl: Without the pressure of, ya
know, everyone watching.

C-Note: So why didn't you call me?

C-Note: For example, like when I called
you? Last weekend?

He had a point. I did need to explain that.

TrumpetGrrl: Sorry. I was visiting a friend.

C-Note: Oh.

I felt a sudden urge to justify myself.

TrumpetGrrl: Alex ... who I met at Covington. Remember?

C-Note: Oh, right. "Alex."

TrumpetGrrl: WTF are the quotes supposed to mean, smartass?

He didn't reply, and I took a minute to breathe in deeply,
willing the anger to seep out of my bloodstream. I knew

exactly what he meant by the quotes. He thought Alex was someone I had cheated on him with. And just because I sort of *had*, didn't mean he could say it. But at the same time, it also didn't mean I could be angry with him for implying.

Right?

TrumpetGrrl: ???
C-Note: Nothing. Sorry I brought it up.
C-Note: Anyway.
TrumpetGrrl: Anyway.
C-Note: You did good in band today.

Half the anger melted away with just that one comment. He knew how much that meant to me.

TrumpetGrrl: Thanks ... you really think so?
C-Note: Yeah. I mean, started out a bit rough, but you handled it well. How do you feel about it?
TrumpetGrrl: Good. Really good, actually.
C-Note: Cool.
TrumpetGrrl: I think I'm still going to go for that State scholarship.
C-Note: Oh yeah? I thought you always planned to do that.
TrumpetGrrl: Well, I sort of let it fall

BY THE WAYSIDE ... THOUGHT I HAD CHANGED
PLANS AND WAS GOING TO COVINGTON AFTER ...
EVERYTHING.

"Everything" being the fact he broke my heart, but I didn't
think I needed to elaborate on that.

C-NOTE: I SEE.
TRUMPETGRRL: BUT, UM ... HERE'S MY PROB-
LEM.
TRUMPETGRRL: I SORT OF NEED HELP.
C-NOTE: OH? WITH WHAT?

Ugh, this was going to be harder than I thought. Is there
anything worse than asking for help from someone who
rejected you?

No. That's what I thought.

But Alex's words came back to me, about how I never
let anyone help me. Connor had allegedly still wanted to
be my friend, and this was a way that a friend could help
another friend, so it was perfectly reasonable of me to ask.
Right?

I typed it all out as quickly as possible.

TRUMPETGRRL: I WAS HOPING YOU'D HELP ME.
TRUMPETGRRL: WITH GETTING THE SOLO INTO
SHAPE.

His reply came after a long pause.

C-Note: Um ... I see.

Which was pretty much the most crazy-making way he could have replied. Good job, Connor.

TrumpetGrrl: So?
C-Note: You really want to spend time around me? After everything?
TrumpetGrrl: No, I'm just using you for your skillz.
TrumpetGrrl: That's a joke, by the way.
C-Note: Oh ... ha.
TrumpetGrrl: Please ... you're the only one I can think of who can get me through this.
C-Note: Really?
TrumpetGrrl: Really.
C-Note: Hmm ... what piece are you playing again?

And for a few minutes it was like nothing had ever changed, like it was us from a few months ago, talking and laughing and teasing online. He made fun of the piece I'd chosen, I made fun of him for not knowing what he was talking about. It was kind of creepy, actually, when I stopped to think about it.

I mean, all of this shit had happened and we were pretending like it hadn't. We'd yelled at each other in the middle of the hotel at prom. He'd said he didn't love me anymore.

Yet we were … joking around?

Well, whatever. Probably best not to think about it.

TrumpetGrrl: So … you'll help me?
TrumpetGrrl: I mean, you don't HAVE to.
TrumpetGrrl: But it'd be really cool.
C-Note: Hmm … what do I get in return?

I sat back in my chair, blinking at the screen. And just what the hell was that supposed to mean? Because that was the sort of thing he used to say before when he wanted to make out.

TrumpetGrrl: Um, my eternal gratitude?
C-Note: Hmm … I guess that will have to do.
TrumpetGrrl: Great! So, tomorrow?
C-Note: Tomorrow what?
TrumpetGrrl: You help me with the solo, dumb boy.
C-Note: Yeah, I suppose I can …
TrumpetGrrl: And then maybe the next day? And the day after that?
C-Note: Dude, how behind are you?
C-Note: And aren't you some sort of trumpet goddess anyway? Why do you need my help?

TRUMPETGRRL: UM ... BECAUSE.

C-NOTE: BECAUSE WHAT?

TRUMPETGRRL: BECAUSE YOU'RE THE ONLY ONE
WHO CAN HELP ME.

Then I took a deep breath and said what I really didn't
want to say.

TRUMPETGRRL: AND I'M SCARED AND I DON'T
THINK I CAN DO IT ALONE.

His response came right away, as if that's what he was waiting to hear.

C-NOTE: OKAY.

Twenty-seven

The next day, Connor came over to my house after school to practice. We met by my car fifteen minutes after school was out since I wasn't exactly excited about the idea of everyone knowing about our arrangement.

Even though it's likely no one would care, anyway.

The people who would probably care, Jake and Kristen, I was especially careful around. I was pretty sure Kristen would try to beat me up if I told her I was hanging around with Connor again, and Jake would probably end up on the floor laughing hysterically. Everyone else would make all sorts of judgments and I just didn't want to deal with any of it.

So, it became sort of like it was when we first started dating in the fall. Covert.

"Um, is all this really necessary?" Connor asked, breaking an uncomfortable silence as I started up the car.

"Yes," I said. "What, do you mind or something?"

He shrugged. "I don't know. Are you embarrassed by me again?"

"Again?" I asked innocently.

He looked over at me and grinned. "Yeah, again. Just like old times, huh?"

And I smiled back at him. We both laughed and I almost forgot he had been such a terrible person to me. Almost, but not quite.

We went back to my house and set up in the living room. Though I normally practiced in my room, it would have been entirely too strange to be in there alone with Connor.

The last time we'd been in my room, which had been a month ago when my parents were out for the evening, we had *not* been practicing trumpet. If you know what I mean.

I got my trumpet out of the case and handed him a copy of the sheet music.

"So...how do you want to do this?" He spread it out on my music stand. "You want me to, like, stop you if you do something wrong?"

"Well, I just want to run through it and...yeah. If some part sucks, I want you to tell me."

I regretted asking him that within a few bars.

"That's supposed to be staccato," he broke in, right as I was getting into the groove of the piece.

"What?" I said irritably, taking my trumpet away from my lips.

"Right there," he said, pointing to a place in the music. "Staccato. You weren't really doing that."

"I know it's staccato," I snapped. "And I was playing it that way."

"Well, hey," he said, shaking his head and putting his hands up. "I guess you don't need my help then."

"Ugh," I said, and took a deep breath. "Yes, I do need your help. Okay. Staccato. I'll try again."

I made it a few more bars in before he stopped me again. "That's a crescendo. You see it, right?"

"Yes!" I said. He raised his eyebrows at me. "I mean, yes, I do. Thanks for pointing it out."

And so the practice session went. It was rather painful, actually, like dissecting a particularly annoying algebra formula or mapping out a Shakespearean sonnet.

Connor was a tough critic, no doubt about it. He didn't let me get away with anything.

"Nope, do it again," he'd say when I forgot the staccato notes or the crescendos or the phrasing he'd suggested.

And I'd briefly fantasize about throwing my trumpet at his head and ripping up the music, flinging it up in the air as I stormed out of there. But then I reminded myself that he was doing exactly what I'd asked him to do, exactly what I needed him to do.

I'd never really let him help me before. His musical talent was something we hadn't discussed much when we were dating, because he was still embarrassed that he had quit his old performing arts high school and I was a bit insecure over the fact he was (technically) better than me at trumpet.

But now I was thanking my lucky stars he was better. I wanted that State scholarship.

And that fact that we weren't dating, which probably made him less afraid of criticizing me, made it even more productive.

"Okay, dude, my lips are shot," I said an hour later.

"Wuss," he muttered, and then grinned and looked to see how I was reacting.

"Punk kid," I said back.

"Control freak," he said.

"Brat," I replied, jabbing my elbow sharply into his side.

Connor laughed, lightly pushing me away, his hands warm on my arm. I looked up at his face. His smile faded.

"I should go," he said abruptly, sitting down and cramming his feet into his shoes.

"Um, okay," I said. "Do you want a—"

"No, I'll walk."

"Are you sure? It's no—"

"Yeah, I'm sure." He was already halfway to the front door.

"Well, thanks," I said. "For your help and all."

"No problem," he said, hand on the doorknob. "Um…
do you want to practice again?" He opened the door and
looked about two seconds from fleeing.

I glanced at the music, trying to judge how I felt about
it. "Since the recital is this weekend, um…yeah, I would
like some more…help."

"Okay," he said. "Tomorrow, then."

I was still standing in the middle of the living room,
staring at the door, when my mom came in several minutes later. I quickly grabbed my stuff and headed for my
room.

"Hi honey," she said, juggling some bags. "Was that
Connor I saw walking down the street?"

"Who?" I said, folding up the music as if I hadn't heard
her. I just didn't want to dissect the whole situation with
her.

Mom narrowed her eyes at me. "It was Connor, wasn't
it?"

"Oh, right. He's helping me with…something."

"Oh, really," she said, putting down the bags and crossing her arms. "With what, exactly?"

"The solo recital, Mom," I replied, rolling my eyes.
"What did you think?"

"That's it?"

"Jeez, Mother," I said. "Yes."

I walked past her toward the stairs and heard her sigh.
I looked guiltily back. She was rubbing the back of her
neck, looking tired and…old.

Sometimes I forget how old my parents are.

"Sorry," I said. " I didn't mean to snap."

She looked up at me, surprised.

"Oh," she said. "Well, I'm just trying to stay updated on your life, that's all."

"I know."

"I just can't believe you're going to be gone in a few months." Mom shook her head sadly. "The house is going to feel so empty."

I put down my stuff, walked over to her, and hugged her.

"I know, Mom ... I'll miss you guys too."

I felt her tense in surprise, and then she hugged me back.

The next day, directing the band went even better. The class sat down in their seats without me needing to yell, and I even felt like maybe I'd helped the flute section figure out a tough part in one of the pieces.

I mean, they basically figured it out by themselves, but I was on the podium when they did it.

In the car that afternoon, Connor told me that I'd done a good job. Again.

"Really?"

"Yeah, I mean, I can totally see you doing that as your career," he said. "Can't you?"

"I'm starting to be able to," I said. "I mean, before it just seemed like something that would be cool to do because I couldn't really think of anything else that would be as cool. But now it seems like something I might love to do. And be good at."

"That's great, Ellie. I'm happy for you."

We rode in a semi-comfortable silence for a minute, and then he spoke.

"So does this mean you're definitely going to State? For the Music Ed program?"

"I'm not sure," I said. "It might."

"What happened to Covington?" he asked.

I shrugged. "I thought I had decided, but somewhere along the line the decision changed. Or became less clear. Or...something."

"I see," he said. I glanced at him and he looked confused.

"You do?" I asked.

He was silent for a moment. "It was really hard for me to think about you going away, you know?"

I glanced over at him again and, for some reason, my stomach turned over. I wasn't sure I was ready to have the whole breakup-dissection discussion with Connor just yet. Maybe in a few months or, preferably, the tenth of *never*.

But I couldn't get mad. He was helping me, after all. I had to give him something.

"Um...sure?" I said.

"When you got all excited about going there, and it

seemed like such a good place for you, I … " he trailed off. "And you'd made friends there already and I could see you having this whole life without me."

I had no idea what to say. So I settled for "Okay."

Connor was on a roll, though, apparently not noticing my discomfort.

"And you came back and you were different. I don't know what happened and I don't really want to know. But whatever it was made it clear that … " he stopped.

"That what?" I said after a few moments.

"That you didn't need me."

"Uh, do I have to remind you that you broke up with me?" I said. "You're the one who said you didn't love me anymore." Just repeating those words out loud in the presence of the person who said them made me feel nauseous.

"I know I said that," he said quietly.

"So I don't know why you're blaming it all on me," I continued. My heart was pounding in the back of my throat, my vision blurring ever so slightly as it always did when I was on the verge of being overemotional. "I didn't *want* to break up … things were weird, but I wanted to figure it out. You're the one who ended it."

"I know," he said again, even more quietly.

I pulled into the driveway feeling raw and exposed and vaguely blindsided. I had not been expecting this conversation. I told Connor that.

"Sorry," he said, not looking at me. "It's not like I

planned it. Just sort of happened. I hate not being able to talk to you."

We sat in the car for a minute, the air inside getting warmer and stuffier, neither of us willing to be the next person to talk. It felt like one of those moments when whatever was said next could be a really big deal.

Unless I made it not a big deal.

"I guess we should go in," I finally said.

"Okay."

We ran through my solo a couple of times, and never brought up what was said in the car. We barely even looked at each other. Something in our previous day's peace had changed.

"Well, you sound fine," he said after I complained that my lip was giving out. "I don't think you need anymore help, really. When do you meet with your accompanist?"

"Tomorrow, and then Saturday afternoon," I told him. "Oh, by the way, my parents are having a sort of open house thing after the recital. If, you know, you think you might want to come."

"Okay," he said.

"Mr. Barr said he was coming," I said. "And, um, you know. Free food and all. You totally don't have to, though, it's kind of silly and I don't know if it'd be weird but—"

"Ellie," he broke in, putting his hand on my shoulder and smiling. "You're babbling. It's cool. I'll come."

I smiled back. There was a long moment as we just looked at each other, standing close like we used to do. For the first time since we broke up, I thought that I could smell him … that mix of his minty shampoo and deodorant and detergent that was still so familiar it was like looking at the back of my own hand.

"Okay," I said slowly, unable to break my eyes away from his. "That's great."

"Okay," he repeated. For a moment it seemed like he was leaning in toward me, but then he blinked quickly and looked down at his feet.

"Anyway, I should get home and do some … uh … homework or something," he said.

"All right," I said, and immediately began biting my thumbnail.

He looked back up at me, like he was suppressing a laugh.

"What?" I said.

"You're biting your nails."

"So?"

"You only do that when you're freaking out," he said.

"I'm not freaking out," I told him, putting my hand in my pocket to keep it away from my mouth.

"Sure," he said, rolling his eyes.

"I'm not!" I insisted.

"Whatever," he said.

"I'm totally not!" I said, and reached out to playfully poke him in the stomach.

He grabbed my hand and held on, a little tighter than strictly necessary. I laughed and looked up at his face.

And suddenly it was like right before we started dating, right before we were a "we." When every touch was unexpected, heady, sharp as lightning.

And then he dropped my hand, scratched the back of his head, and said, "Okay, I really have to go. Bye."

I watched him walk out the door, and I smiled.

Twenty-eight

That night, I was trying to wrangle my mind into concentrating on AP European History instead of Connor's face when Alex called me. I picked up the phone without really considering it.

"Um, hello?" I said. We hadn't spoken since the hotel incident.

"Hey, Ellie," she said, sounding as uncomfortable as I felt. "What's up?"

We talked around things for a few minutes, sticking to the unweird stuff like how Alex was finishing up her finals and my AP tests and graduation.

"So your recital is this weekend?" she asked. "Do you feel ready?"

"Sort of," I said, thinking of Connor. For some reason

it seemed like a bad idea to tell Alex about his involvement. Especially at this fragile stage in my relationship with both of them.

"Listen," she said. "I just wanted to say I'm sorry about how it went last weekend. I know it ended up being strange and I hate that and I want things to be cool between us."

I blinked for a moment, not sure what to say. Then I went the coward's route.

"Things are cool," I lied. "I'm not sure what you're worrying about."

"Um..." there was a confused pause. "They're cool? What about... you know?"

"What? The fact we were drunk and silly and then the next morning we were hungover and cranky?"

"Hmm," Alex said. "That's an interesting way to frame it."

I sighed. "I don't know, dude. I'm not even sure what happened, you know? Or why things got so strange..."

"I know, neither do I!" Alex said. "It was like totally fine and then it just wasn't and I hate that!"

"Me too," I said.

"So you think we can make it cool again?" she asked. "Just by saying it's cool?"

"Um, sure," I said. "Why not?"

"Okay good," she said. "I'm really relieved."

"I am too," I said, though I wasn't entirely sure. I had missed her, I guess, but it had also been kind of nice not to have that weirdness, nor to deal with any of her pressure to go to Covington.

"Because I'm going to have a surprise for you," she said.

"What's that?"

"It's a surprise, duh," she said. "You'll have to wait and see."

"All right," I said, shrugging at my empty room. All the surprises that came with being Alex's friend could be kind of exhausting.

We talked for a few minutes more and then she said she had to go.

"Thanks for calling," I said. "It was nice to talk to you again."

"Yeah, you too," she said. "See you soon!"

"Huh?"

"See you soon!" she repeated, and then hung up.

I looked at the phone in my hand. *See you soon?* What was that supposed to mean? I hoped it didn't mean she was going to show up here.

I didn't have time to puzzle over it, though. Especially since I was distracted by a fight with my parents when I went downstairs to get a study-break snack.

They were sitting in the living room with glasses of wine, looking like they were in the middle of a very important discussion. I immediately regretted showing my face.

"Ellie, the deposit to Covington is due," my mom said

out of nowhere, as she'd been saying almost every day since we'd visited the campus.

"I know Mom," I said, rolling my eyes. "I told you that I'm going to send it in after the solo recital."

"But why wait?" Dad asked. "We thought you'd decided on Covington."

I hadn't told my parents about conducting the band for Mr. Barr. They wouldn't even really understand what it meant, anyway, plus it'd just make them stress out about my college choice some more. Basically, it was something I'd rather just discuss after the fact.

"Maybe," I said, and didn't elaborate further.

Then Mom went off on her worrywart rant about what if they gave my place away? What if I didn't get the music scholarship and decided I didn't want to go to State? What if I ended up living at home with them until I was thirty-two? What *then?*

"Mom, chill out," I said. "Covington's deadline isn't until the end of next week. It's going to be fine."

But she kept going and going, and then started stressing about the party on Saturday after the recital and finally I just had to escape.

"Where are you going?" Mom called after me.

"I have to practice," I said over my shoulder. "And you're driving me kind of crazy."

"Elaine," Dad called, but I was already halfway up the stairs.

"Can we just talk about it later?" I called back.

Neither of them answered, so I took that as a yes and escaped into my room.

Mr. Barr was back the next day, and I stopped to talk to him before school even started.

"How did directing go?" he asked, smiling. "The sub left a good report."

I shrugged and bit my lip. "Well, it started out kind of hard, but then it got better. I think."

He squinted at me.

"You think?"

"It seems like a really ... hard job," I said. "I didn't really realize. Like, what kind of energy doing that kind of thing takes, I guess."

Mr. Barr nodded. "That's true. It's not something you really can understand without doing it."

"Yeah, totally!" I said.

"Did it help you come to any sort of decision?" he asked.

"I think so ... " I said. "Maybe? I don't know."

"But you were hoping it would, right?"

"Yeah." I sighed. "I was hoping it would be kind of like a big booming voice out of the sky telling me what to do."

Mr. Barr is so cool he didn't even have to ask what the hell I meant by that. He just nodded.

"It wasn't," I said. "No booming voice, I mean."

"I see." Mr. Barr paused. "But Connor tells me you two have been working on your senior solo recital piece?"

I felt my cheeks go warm. Connor had been talking about me to Mr. Barr!

"Yeah," I said. "I needed help on it, and he is, you know, really good and all."

"He sure is," Mr. Barr said. "I'm glad you're friends again."

I looked down at my feet, embarrassed.

"Me too."

He changed the subject and we talked for a while more about the senior solo recital and band in general, and as I left his office I was overwhelmed with pre-graduation nostalgia.

Pretty soon I wouldn't have Mr. Barr to talk to every day... pretty soon I'd be surrounded by strangers in some strange place.

During band, I took my place back at the top of the trumpet section. Connor nudged me with his elbow and leaned over to whisper in my ear.

"Slumming it with the common folk?"

I giggled and tapped his knee with the bell of my trumpet, then saw that Jake was staring at us.

"What the hell?" he mouthed at me. I shrugged back when Connor wasn't looking, but the damage was done.

I was accosted by Kristen in the hall outside the cafeteria.

"Okay, spill," she demanded. "What is going on with you and Connor?"

Seriously, it was like reliving the beginning of that relationship all over again. And, like last time, I totally lied.

"Nothing," I said. "So, hey, you're coming to my party on Saturday, right?"

"Don't even try to change the subject," she spat back, glaring. "And yes, I am. But back to the more important issue, and that's Connor ... what's going on? Jake saw you two looking all couple-y again. Care to share?"

"Not really," I said, trying to get around her into the cafeteria.

"Are you two dating again?" she asked, ever persistent.

"No," I said.

"Are you sure?"

"Yes," I said. "He helped me out with my solo and we're getting along again."

"But what—" she started, and I broke in.

"Kris, it's not a big deal," I said. "Seriously. Can we please just go eat? I'm starving."

"Fine." She pouted.

Connor was sitting at our lunch table again. He looked up at me timidly, his eyes obviously searching for my approval and permission. And involuntarily, I grinned back. Which was all the information that he and everyone at the table needed.

I really wished I'd started making it a routine to go out to lunch. Seriously.

Twenty-nine

I woke up on Saturday, the day of the solo recital, with a grim feeling of foreboding in my stomach. It felt like another one of those days where the direction of my life might be determined—and, you know, that's kind of stressful. Especially when you can see it coming in a head-on-collision track. And I seemed to be having a lot of those days lately.

Mom was in full-on panic mode in the kitchen, stirring a giant bowl of pasta salad for the party. Dad was in the living room, trying to figure out how to use the vacuum. My parents weren't much for party throwing (or cleaning) and this was a big deal for them.

I tiptoed around Mom to get a bowl of cereal, then headed back to my room. I paused along the way to show

Dad how the vacuum turned on—vacuuming had been one of my household chores for years and I couldn't remember the last time I'd seen him with a cleaning product in hand.

"Thanks, honey," he said, looking flustered.

"Are you sure you don't want me to do that?" I asked over the whir of the motor. "I really don't mind."

"No, no," he said. "You go relax. It's your big day. We'll get it all ready."

He promptly sucked a corner of the curtain into the vacuum, but waved me away when I tried to help.

While I ate my cereal I tooled around online, checking to see what people were up to. I noticed that Alex had changed her Facebook status to "Road Trip!" and frowned at a twinge of jealousy that burned through me.

Road trip? Weird. And why didn't she tell me about it when we talked online last night? It was probably some spontaneous thing like what we had done last weekend. Probably with someone more interesting than me, who didn't freak out all the time.

Except, maybe she meant she was coming to see ... me? Maybe the "see you soon" had literally meant that she'd see me soon ...

Then I rolled my eyes at myself and clicked a new page. All that wondering about what Alex was doing was exhausting and I just didn't have the energy. I sort of didn't even care anymore.

I idly clicked over to Connor's profile to see if he had

updated anything. I had re-friended him last night after he had made fun of me for un-friending him after prom.

"Well, you couldn't expect me to just keep you as a friend," I had pointed out.

We had been sitting in our corner of the park last night, close to the place where we had met just over a month ago in the dead of night. The plan had been to throw a Frisbee around, but it lay lonely at our feet, unthrown.

"No, I guess not," he said, avoiding my eye. "Not after … that."

I opened my mouth, and then closed it again. Was this the time for that post-breakup dissection?

Then he leaned into me hard, pushing me off balance so I almost toppled over. That was the answer. Which was no, it was not time.

"Jackass!" I said, and got up to where I was kneeling so I could push hard with both hands.

"Hey!" he said, falling over dramatically.

"Get what you deserve, dude," I said.

We half-wrestled for a few moments, his hands creeping familiarly over me, which I only lightly pushed away. In the end, he was lying on the ground and I was leaning over him, holding his wrists down. Even though he could probably have thrown me off, he stayed there, looking up at me.

I stared back, my brain churning. It felt exactly like it had the last time we were in the park, the night we had snuck out.

"What?" he said, softly. "Why are you looking at me like that?"

I didn't know what to say, so I didn't say anything.

Slowly he drew his wrists down to his sides, which forced me to lean down farther and farther so pretty soon my face was right above his.

"What?" he said again, even softer, then lifted his head to kiss me.

I let him for a few moments, drowning in the familiarity of having him close, his breath on my cheek, the stubble on his chin scratching at my jaw. I let go of his wrists and he wrapped his arms around me so my weight rested on him.

I almost started crying, even as I kissed him. I'd thought that I'd never kiss him again, that we'd never be this close. And yet here we were like nothing had changed.

But it *had* changed. I couldn't forget about when he said: *I don't think I love you anymore.* There was no excuse for that.

I drew away from him and sat back up on my knees. He blinked at me from the ground.

"What?" he said again, this time much less seductively. "What's wrong with you?"

I opened my mouth to say *No, things cannot just go back to the way they were* and *You were mean and cruel and awful to me and how can you expect me to just allow you to kiss me and be fine about it?* and *No, I have moved on. I am over this. I don't need you.*

But instead, I said, "I need to go home. Mom needs help."

God, I'm such a big fat chicken.

He sat up. "Um, okay. I guess."

"Sorry," I said, and could have kicked myself as soon as the words were out of my mouth. Why did I owe him an apology? Why I was I saying sorry for sticking to how I felt? *Ugh.*

"It's okay," he said, shrugging, which sort of made me feel like kicking him. Who was he to *forgive* me?

"Anyway…" I said, getting up.

"Ellie, we need to talk," he said abruptly.

"Yeah, I know," I said, gathering up the Frisbee. "But I can't do it now. This isn't the day to deal with this."

He stood up, brushing off his jeans. "When is the day to deal with it?"

Uh, never?

"I don't know," I said, feeling annoyed. "I need a good night's sleep, though."

"Ellie, it's only, like, seven o'clock."

Now I was even more annoyed. "I have to practice, too. And I just need to…"

"Need to what?"

"Be somewhere else," I said, not meeting his eye.

"Oh."

I rolled my eyes. "Come on, I'll drive you home."

In my room the next morning, eating my cereal and

checking Connor's profile online, I saw that he had changed his status from "Single" to "It's Complicated."

I sighed. It was safe to assume that was in reference to me.

I slurped up the rest of my milk and went to brush my teeth. Now was not the time to be obsessing over Connor or Alex or anything except the recital.

Today, my only friend was my trumpet.

I showed up for the recital an hour before it was due to start. All of the soloists were milling around in the band room, even the singers and string instrument players, because it was the closest music room to the auditorium.

I knew a lot of the other senior soloists, but I stuck to myself in the corner of the room, continuously polishing my trumpet even though it was totally smudge free. It was time to be in the zone.

My accompanist, an elderly woman named Mrs. Samson, stopped by to check on me.

"So I suppose this is it, right?" I said. "No more festivals or recitals or anything."

She had accompanied me for recitals and solo and ensemble events since eighth grade, and part of the reason why I loved her so much was her total lack of sentimentality. Mrs. Samson was all business about accompanying, and expected me to be as well.

So I was a little surprised when she put her hand on my shoulder and smiled at me.

"Ellie, it's been a pleasure to work with you over the years," she said. "You've been one of my favorites. Good luck tonight. I'm sure you'll blow them away like you do every time."

I tried valiantly not to, but I totally teared up.

"Thanks," I said. "I'll try."

She squeezed my shoulder and left to talk with someone else she was accompanying.

I wiped my eyes and went back to polishing my trumpet, thinking about how it was all ending so fast. I didn't feel ready... I wanted to stop time. Or at least pause for a minute to really soak in where I was and figure out how I was feeling.

As if on cue, Connor popped in the door of the band room and waved hesitantly at me. I sighed and waved him over.

"Hey," he said. "You look really nice. Isn't that the dress that..."

"Yeah, that I wore for Valentine's Day," I said, with some discomfort. It was both weird and very sweet that he remembered.

"Well, I know you're probably freaking out, so I just wanted to say good luck." He held out his arms, indicating that he wanted to hug me.

"Thanks," I said, standing up and stepping into his

arms. He wrapped them around me and put his face down close to my neck.

"I'm sorry, Ellie," he murmured. "I made a terrible, stupid mistake and I don't want things to be ruined with you forever because I love you. I really love you."

I felt like I had been doused with ice water from head to toe. These were the words I'd been wanting to hear since he broke up with me. And now that they had been said, I wished he would take them back. Or save them for later. Or something, anything, other than telling me this right before I was supposed to go win a scholarship.

I didn't yell at him, though, or get mad. I just carefully disengaged myself from his arms, gave him as much of a smile as I could muster, and crossed my arms.

"We'll talk about this later," I said firmly.

"But—"

"Later. Please."

He deflated like a balloon pricked with a pin. Connor had obviously been envisioning some great romantic reunion, and I had let him down.

"Okay," he said, with one last wounded-puppy look.

I watched him leave, and then I turned to kick the nearest locker with my three-inch heel. Not that hard, mind you, just a tap to get out some of the frustration, but a few prissy choir girls looked over at me in abject fear, as if they thought they might be next.

"Sorry," I said, smiling brightly. "Nerves."

They looked semi-relieved and nodded sympathetically.

The recital started, and one by one the people in the room were called out to the auditorium stage. I was toward the end of the lineup, which really made things worse. Once each person performed, they went to sit in the audience, so no one came back into the band room.

Pretty soon it was just me, some cello player who was wearing white socks with his black suit, and an exchange student from Sweden who played the piano. Neither of them offered any conversation, or maybe it was that I looked scary, pacing up and down with my trumpet in hand, running through the music in my head, trying not to think of Connor.

Finally I was beckoned toward the door and led to the auditorium, where I stepped out onto the familiar stage and into a spotlight. Mrs. Samson was already waiting for me at the piano, smiling slightly. I couldn't make out most the faces in the audience at first, but as I stood unfolding my music on the stand, my eyes gradually adjusted.

I could see the row of my family and friends—Jake and Kristen sitting with my parents, a few other friends from band, and Mr. Barr and his wife sitting at the end with Connor.

Mr. Barr met my eye and subtly nodded toward the woman sitting in front of him. It was Professor Reynolds from State, the head of the scholarship committee, who had come to hear me play.

I took a deep breath, confidence running through my veins as it almost always did when I was about to blast out a piece of music I felt good about. I could do this; I had been practicing to do this since I first picked up a trumpet when I was eleven.

Piece of cake.

I nodded at Mrs. Samson, who rested her fingers on the piano keys. I lifted my trumpet and put it to my lips.

And it was as I was taking a final scan of the audience, to see again just who I would be blasting away, when I saw her staring intently at me with wide eyes, a broad grin on her face. Sitting in the front row.

It was Alex.

I flubbed the first note.

Thirty

After the recital, it was obvious that no one knew what to say to me.

Well, my parents hugged me and said that I did wonderfully, but they don't know anything about music so that didn't count.

Mr. Barr gave me an awkward clap on the shoulder and said that once I got over my nerves, I sounded great. I thanked him with gritted teeth.

Jake and Kristen hugged me and said they'd meet me at the party.

"Don't drive off a bridge on your way home," Kristen said quietly. "We'll talk this through. It'll be okay."

Connor hung back, looking a little fearful, as if he might get blamed for what had happened. Which wasn't a surprise considering I'd blamed him for it happening last time, when I messed up my solo at band camp in August.

Alex was nowhere to be seen.

But I didn't much care. I didn't much care about anything, in fact. I hadn't been expecting to feel this amount of ... *relief.*

It was like the die had been cast. I couldn't take back what had occurred and I couldn't change it or pretend it didn't happen. There was nothing I could do about it, and I couldn't believe how *free* I felt all of a sudden.

Even if, you know, I didn't enjoy flubbing notes and looking like a jackass.

I was looking around the crowd when Professor Reynolds, the director of the scholarship committee, approached me with an apologetic expression.

"Ellie, it was wonderful to finally hear you play, and that was really quite a good performance after the unfortunate beginning," she said.

I nodded and tried to look concerned. I already knew what she was going to tell me. I had known since the second I flubbed the note that I wouldn't win the scholarship. That I didn't particularly deserve it.

"And I know you were hoping to hear good news about the alumni scholarship, and while we certainly will be lucky to have you in the department, for this very competitive award I'm afraid ... " she trailed off, a forced smile on her face.

"I understand," I said, and I meant it. "Thank you for your consideration."

"Of course, my pleasure," she said, looking relieved. "I hope you're still planning to attend State."

I opened my mouth, but there weren't any words in my brain to say anything. Once again, I was unable to see my future.

"I have . . . no idea," I said.

She nodded. "I understand. It's a tough decision. But you are clearly very talented. Mr. Barr told me about how you filled in for him while he was at a conference, and that's very impressive. I'm sure you would make a fine band director."

"Thanks," I said. "I sort of think that I would as well."

She smiled and put her hand on my shoulder. "Wonderful job, Ellie. Congratulations on your accomplishment."

As she walked away, I heard a surprised cough behind me. It was Connor, sidling up like I was a wild animal.

"Hey," I said. "What's up?"

He looked hopeful at my apparent good attitude. "Did she just say congratulations because she offered you the scholarship?"

"Dude, what do you think?" I asked. "You heard what happened."

"Um . . . you got the scholarship anyway?"

"No," I said, biting my pinky-nail. "No, I didn't."

"Oh."

"Yeah."

"Well, so what happened?" he asked. "With the first note, I mean."

I briefly considered getting snippy and yelling at him for being insensitive, but I just didn't have the energy. Nor did I care. It was over. There was nothing I could do about it now.

"I don't know," I said, shrugging. "Guess I screwed up. Wasn't meant to be."

Connor blinked at me for a few seconds, as if suspecting I had lost my mind. "I . . . see."

"Yeah, maybe it's not such a big deal," I said. Which is when I looked over and saw that Alex was standing with my parents, talking animatedly.

"Shit," I said softly.

"What?" Connor looked around. "Who's that with your parents?"

"Um, never mind, I'll tell you later," I said quickly. "So, looks like Mr. Barr is waiting for you over there. See you at the party?"

I gave his arm a small push.

"Okay," he said, confused, walking away.

Alex was dressed in a pleated pink cotton skirt and several layers of white tank tops, her hair pulled up in pigtails like the last time I saw her. She was grinning up at my dad as if he had just said the funniest thing ever (which, as his daughter, I can assure you he had not), and both my parents were smiling fondly at her.

"Ellie, we have to get home to get things ready," Mom called over to me. "You'll give Alex directions, right?"

I nodded silently as they left.

Alex turned and looked at me, then bounded toward me with open arms.

"Ellie!" she squealed, hugging me. "That was awesome! I mean, I knew you'd be awesome but that was awesomer than the awesome I imagined!"

She smelled like the Strawberry Shortcake doll I had when I was a kid.

I let myself enjoy being hugged for two seconds before discomfort exploded inside of me. Who was this girl? Why was she even here? There weren't many people left in the school foyer, but what if they wondered what was going on?

"Thanks," I said, disengaging from her.

"What's wrong?" she said, her brow furrowed. "Are you okay?"

"I screwed it up, Alex," I said. "I screwed up that first note and didn't get the scholarship."

"Oh," she said softly, putting her hand on my arm. "Um...I don't know what to say."

"You don't have to say anything," I said. "I'd prefer it that way, anyhow."

Both of us stared at the ground for a moment. Alex took her hand away.

"Well, aren't you surprised to see me?" she asked, striking a little pose with her hands on her hips.

"Sure," I said. "I mean, it was cool of you to drive so far just for a stupid recital."

"It wasn't stupid." She punched my shoulder lightly. "I'm glad I got to see you play."

"Right. I'm … glad you did too."

"Your parents said you're having a party now," she said. "Do you mind if I come?"

Although the idea of having her and Connor in the same vicinity and possibly talking to each other was most horrifying, I nodded. There was nothing else I could do. She had driven all this way and it was only polite.

Alex followed me home in the little silver Jetta she'd gotten from her parents when she graduated high school. I kept glancing in the rearview mirror, at her head bopping in time to some unheard music. Instead of obsessing over my solo, I thought about how different she was from me.

Alex and Covington were a different world.

I drummed my steering wheel in time with the swing CD I was playing on my car stereo. The trumpets wailing out the melody made me smile.

Now that the scholarship was out of the picture, it would seem like the decision to join the Alex/Covington world should be easier, right?

Then why didn't it feel that way?

A bunch of cars were parked near my house. My most favorite people were inside, waiting to celebrate with me. Well, more like commiserate in this instance, though I was glad they were there all the same.

But when I parked my car in the driveway, I had to sit there for a minute, trying to talk myself out of starting up the car again and driving away until everyone left.

There was a knock on my window. I looked over, expecting Alex to be smiling cheerfully at me, but it was Mom and Dad.

"Ellie?" my mom said. "Are you getting out?"

I shrugged. "I guess."

"Dad and I want to talk to you before you go in, okay?"

"All right," I said with a sigh, and opened the door.

They stood in front of me, Dad's arm around Mom's waist, obviously trying to present a united front.

"Sweetheart, we know about the scholarship," Mom said. "Connor told us."

I bit my lip and leaned against my car, then said, "Well, how nice of him to share."

"He was worried, Ellie." Dad reached over to stroke my hair the way he used to do when I was small and scared of thunderstorms. "And we're worried, too. We know you must be disappointed."

I could feel my lip trembling. I'd thought that I wasn't upset, that I was fatalistic and able to accept the whole deal, but something about my parents' sympathy made me want to go hide under the shrubs in the front yard the way I did when I was eight.

"Yeah, I guess I am," I said, not looking at them because I knew that would mean instant tears. "Well, I'm confused."

They both nodded, urging me on.

"I wanted that scholarship so that I wouldn't have to bother you or anyone for anything," I said. "It was like a sign that I was making the right choice. And a chance to be an adult."

"You don't need to worry about that yet, honey," said Dad. "We're here to help you, you know. That's our job."

He looked over at Mom, giving her a little nod like *your turn now.*

"Ellie, you know we have a savings account for you for college," she said. "Your grandparents left you some money and we saved and, you know, you'll still need to get a job for spending money but we can figure out a way to get things to work no matter where you want to go. You're very fortunate to have that and we're not sure why you're so dead set against accepting our help."

"But don't you want me to go to Covington?" I asked in a small voice. "Won't you be mad if I use the money to go to State?"

They looked at each other and had a silent conversation with their eyes. At times like this, it came through just how well my parents knew each other, how long they'd been together.

I wondered if I'd ever find someone with whom I could have an entire discussion without talking. Maybe someday.

"No, sweetheart, we won't be mad," Dad said. "We want you to be happy."

"And if studying to be a band director is what will

make you happy," Mom said slowly, as if the words were sticking a bit in her throat, "then that is what will make us happy."

And those, it turns out, were the words I had been waiting for.

I couldn't help it—I burst into tears. Mom started crying too, of course, and Dad enveloped us both in a big hug and for a few moments we were a solid little three-person unit of family.

And with both my parents' arms around me, all the craziness and irrationality of high school and my soon-to-be-over teenage years began to melt away, just a bit.

Not entirely, but enough so that I could finally see that someday we would be real friends. We were three people with a shared history, even if they didn't understand me completely, and we loved each other.

I'm so lucky. I can never forget that.

Thirty-one

$\mathcal{E}$veryone was quiet and shifty-eyed as I walked into my own party. Which was predictable, I guess, since they probably thought I was on the verge of a full-on meltdown.

Mr. and Mrs. Barr were there, standing with Connor and Kristen and Jake. Aaron and a few other kids from band were huddled around the food table, whispering, and neighbors and family friends who had been at the recital or had been filled in by witnesses wouldn't meet my eye.

It sort of felt like a funeral.

"Hey everyone!" I said brightly to the silent room. "Thanks for sitting through that atrocity. But where's the music? Let's get this party started."

Everyone stared at me as if I'd just spoken in Elvish.

"What's wrong?" I said, to the room in general.

"Are you okay?" Jake asked softly, as my parents came in behind me.

"Yeah," I said. "I totally am."

"Are you sure?" Kristen asked, looking like she wanted to put a hand on my head to check if I had a fever.

"Yes, I'm fine. And actually, I have an announcement to make," I said. "I've finally made a decision about college."

Kristen, Jake, and Connor all gaped at me. Alex's head came into view from the kitchen where she had apparently been hiding. And suddenly, the nervousness took over.

I felt my mom put a hand on my shoulder, and was buoyed.

"Even though I didn't get the scholarship, I'm going to State, guys," I said. "I'm going to be a band director."

The room was silent, and then Mr. Barr took charge of the situation. "Let's all give Ellie a round of applause for that fantastic performance and for her wonderful future as a band director!"

The clapping was hesitant at first, but gradually built up as I smiled at everyone to show them I wasn't upset, that this was what I wanted. Aaron hooted loudly, Kristen was jumping up and down, and Connor was smiling broadly.

I glanced over at the kitchen, but Alex's head had disappeared.

Kristen bounced up to me and squealed, "Next year is going to be so awesome!"

Jake elbowed me in the side and said, "I knew you'd come around."

The room dissolved into individual conversations and people came by to congratulate me and say they were excited for me. When the muscles in my face began to feel like they were going to shatter from too much smiling, I slipped away to find Alex.

She wasn't anywhere downstairs, nor out in the backyard. Her car was still parked on the street, so I knew she hadn't left. Finally I checked my bedroom. She was sprawled across my neatly made bed, facedown.

"Alex?" I said hesitantly, awkward in my own bedroom. "Are you ... okay?"

It was weird to see her there. Weird and kind of violating.

"You're not coming to Covington," she mumbled into my comforter.

"Um, no," I said. "Turns out I'm not."

"Why?" she said.

"I don't think it's my place," I said. "I just don't think it's where I'm meant to be."

"But you didn't get that scholarship," she said, still into my blanket. "I thought if you didn't get it, you weren't going to go there."

A bit of electricity whipped through me.

"What?" I said, carefully.

Alex raised her head and I could see her face was red, as if she had been crying.

"I thought you wouldn't go if you screwed up your solo."

I stared at her.

"Is that why you came?" I finally said. "Did you come to ... screw me up?"

"What? No!" she said, sitting up. "Why would you think that?"

"Well, that's the implication of what you just said. I mean, it sounds like you drove here in order to distract me in the audience so I'd ... mess up my solo? Dude, that is so not cool!"

"No, Ellie, I didn't mean it like that," she said, giving me a disgusted expression and propping herself up on her elbows. "Of course I didn't. Wow, you certainly have a warped view of the world."

"Oh, do I?" I said, crossing my arms.

We glared at each other for a moment. I could hear music playing downstairs, and wished that I were there instead of up here.

"What *are* you doing in Winslow?" I finally asked.

"I came to support my friend," she spat back. "But perhaps I don't have one."

"Perhaps not."

I was tired of how I felt around Alex, like she was one step ahead of me, like she had some dibs on coolness and that I was somehow lucky to know her. She had sort of manipulated it to be that way. She had flattered and sort of wooed me, but when it came down to it, I was just supposed to be a mirror to reflect her awesomeness.

"Remember what you said to me about manipulation?"

I asked. "How if you feel like you're being manipulated, it doesn't matter if the other person intends it or not?"

"Yeah, so?" she said.

"I feel like I'm being manipulated."

"God, whatever, Ellie." She rolled her eyes. "That's so immature."

"Is it?" I said.

"Yes, and ridiculous."

"You're very strange," I told her. "It's like you were trying to convince me to come to Covington so I could be your little hanger-on or something. So I could just reflect back on you how cool you are. It had nothing to do with what was best for me. It was all about you."

She stared at me, opening and closing her mouth, apparently without words.

I wasn't about to be anyone's mirror. I was pretty okay with my own reflection, thank you very much.

And as soon as I realized that, I felt all the power that Alex had over me drain away, like a receding tidal wave. I was in control of myself again. Which is why I could say what I said next without worrying about how it sounded.

"Alex, it meant a lot to me that you came," I said. "Thanks."

She looked down at her hands.

"I don't think you did any of that on purpose," I continued. "And I'm sorry I won't be coming to Covington in the fall, but I hope we can stay in touch."

She squinted at me. "This sort of sounds like...a breakup speech or something."

I shrugged. "I guess it sort of is."

We looked at each other for a few long moments, her eyes gradually hardening. And then she shrugged too.

"Well, all right then."

"All right," I agreed.

Slowly, she got off my bed and walked toward the door, as if giving me ample chance to call her back. But I didn't.

"See you downstairs, I guess," she said over her shoulder. "I suppose I should eat something before I head back."

"Sure," I said. "Stick around, enjoy yourself."

When the door shut behind her, I threw myself on my bed and stared at the ceiling.

What the hell?

I barely had time to start processing what had just happened when there was a knock on my door.

"Christ, what now?" I muttered out loud. "Who is it?"

"Ellie?" It was Connor. "Can I come in?"

Great, just what I needed.

"Whatever," I said. "Why not?"

"What?" he said, opening the door and peeking inside. "Are you okay? People are wondering where you are."

"I'm fine," I said, sitting up.

"Who is that girl? Who just came down the stairs?"

"That's Alex," I said.

"Oh," he said, looking uncomfortable.

"Yep," I said. "Pretty sure we're not friends anymore."

"Huh, that's strange."

Connor looked at me, and the late-evening sun made his blue eyes glimmer. God, he was so freakin' cute. I didn't think I'd ever get over that.

He must have seen something of what I was thinking, because he walked slowly over, put hands on both my shoulders, and pushed me back until we were both lying on my bed. He pulled me into the curve between his arm and body and nuzzled my hair.

"I'm still your friend," he said into the top of my head. His breath felt damp on my scalp.

"I guess," I said, sort of distracted by the fact that every muscle in my body was uncomfortably tense. Apparently some part of me did not want him this close.

"Ellie," he said. "Just think, it could be like this all the time again. Me and you together."

"I've thought about it," I admitted.

"I was an idiot," he murmured. "I wasn't thinking. I was scared and stupid and I love you."

My muscles tensed even more, if that were possible. *No no no*, this is not what I wanted! I didn't want to be Connor's reflection, either. I didn't want to be anyone's other piece, and I didn't want anyone else to be my extra piece.

I just wanted ... me.

And, carefully, I disentangled myself from Connor and stood up.

"It's too late," I said.

He looked at me, his eyes widening in surprise. He sat up.

"What?" he said.

"We had our chance." I leaned over and kissed him gently on the forehead. "It didn't work out, sweetheart."

He blinked at me.

"I don't understand, you were so mad at me when we broke up and said you wanted to work things out and I thought—"

I held up a hand. "You were right to break up with me," I said. "We're both to blame, or no one is to blame, but it was over. It *is* over."

"But…"

I put my hand in his hair, consciously trying to tuck away the memory of how soft it was on my palm. I stroked his face gently, absorbing the exact feel of the curve of his cheek and the angle of his jaw.

I wouldn't ever touch him like this again. I knew that for certain.

Connor was staring at me with wounded eyes. "But I love you."

"You'll love someone else, too," I said. I stroked his head one last time, and then pulled him off my bed by his arm.

"Come on, let's go have fun."

Epilogue

"You think you're ready for this, dude?" asked Jake from behind me.

I turned around and looked at him, grinning. Like me, he was decked out in a bright green and white uniform with pristine gloves, his shiny silver trumpet in hand.

"Oh I'm ready," I replied, bouncing on my toes. "You, on the other hand ... "

Jake had to slum it with the rest of the marching block until he could try out for drum major at the end of sophomore year. I was giving him plenty of grief about the fact he had to relearn how to march and play at the same time.

He laughed and shoulder-checked me, and I bumped my silver-plumed hat against his in retort.

Thwonk.

Our section leader turned to give us a stern look, but I could see he was repressing a smile. Freshmen were expected to be overexcitable. I could hear Kristen's high-pitched giggle in the alto-sax section right at that moment, in fact.

We were standing in the humid, echo-filled tunnel off the football stadium, waiting for our cue to run on for pre-game for the first football game of State's season. All around us I could hear the murmuring roar of thousands of fans.

Somewhere among them sat my parents, my mom attending her first college football game ever. I'd told them they didn't need to come, that it would be hot and crowded, but they insisted.

"No way we're going to miss this," said Dad. "Besides, State is supposed to have a good team this year."

My heavy wool uniform itched. My muscles were still aching from two straight weeks of full-time college band practice. Sweat was dripping down my back, my hair was plastered to my head, and I was half-convinced I was going to trip and fall when we broke into lockstep near the end of pre-game.

But I'd also never been happier. And I'd never been more convinced that I was in the right place at the right time, doing exactly what I was meant to do.

Ever since the night of my senior solo recital, I hadn't felt any doubt about my decision. And this feeling of pure, anticipatory bliss just before I marched out for the first time just confirmed it.

Jake was watching me as if he could read my mind.

"I take it you're happy to be here, huh?" he said.

"Dude, you don't even know," I replied.

"No, I think I do." He inhaled deeply. "It smells like home here. Mmm, the delicious scent of band."

From the entrance of the tunnel came a shrill whistle. The drum major was calling us to attention. It was time to go.

Over the loudspeaker, the announcer pronounced, "Ladies and gentlemen! Presenting the two-hundred-fifty-five-member State Marching Band! *Band*—take the field!"

A massive wave of cheers and applause rumbled through the tunnel. I closed my eyes, soaking in the moment like it was a warm bath.

Then I took a breath, and opened them again.

© Adam P. Schweigert

Josie Bloss, a third-generation band geek, grew up outside of Lansing, Michigan. She attended the University of Michigan, where she was a member of the best college marching band in the country.

When not mining her high school journals for material and wishing there were marching band options for adults, Josie enjoys theater and karaoke. She lives in Bloomington, Indiana. Visit her online at www.josiebloss.com.